Fallin' for the Alpha of the Streets

K.L. Hall

Dedication
To Y.G.

Author Acknowledgments

If you're reading this right now, welcome to the beginning of my latest novel. I want to make this acknowledgements section all about you, the reader. Almost two dozen novels later and you're still here with me. You may be a vet who has been with me since book one, or you may be a newbie who has never even heard of me before now. Whatever brought you to read this, I just want to say T-H-A-N-K Y-O-U.

I've been in this game for five years, and I've never felt more loved than I do now. Your support means so much to a small-town girl like me. Alright, now go ahead and turn the page and get swept up into the love story of Pharaoh and Savannah.

All my love,

KL Hall

Fallin' for the Alpha of the Streets Synopsis

One of the most dangerous things anyone can do with their life is go undercover. But when FBI Special Agent Savannah McKinney gets pulled into Operation November to take down one of Chicago's biggest drug kingpins and notorious gang member, Pharaoh Blackwell, she's up for the challenge.

Pharaoh is six-five, sexy, strapped with a pistol on his hip, and an even deadlier smile. In a profession where everyone wants to take over the streets, his only focus is stacking his money, gaining more power, and commanding respect. Nowhere in that equation did he have time for love, that is, until Savannah crosses his path.

When an unforeseen accident causes her to lose her memory, she winds up falling right into the arms of the man she's supposed to be taking down. Savannah soon finds herself wanting to know everything about the man behind the gruesome murders and the drugs flooding the streets of Chiraq. As the two become closer, it's only a matter of time before their connection becomes increasingly personal—and deadly. Fate brought them together, but will the law or her recollection tear them apart?

Epigraph

"Love will come
And when love comes
Love will hold you
Love will call your name
And you will melt…"

-Rupi Kaur

Prologue

PHARAOH "RO" BLACKWELL

Ominous black clouds covered the sky as heavy rain fell. My heart pounded hard inside my chest while I watched the windshield wipers swish back and forth across the windshield at a rapid pace. A loud clap of thunder rattled, and lightning flashed across the night sky. I looked to my left and studied Frenchie's face. He wore a grim look and had a half-lit blunt hanging off the side of his lip and one hand on the wheel. The speedometer read 110 miles per hour.

"Fuck," I mumbled while looking out of the rearview mirror.

There were dozens of flashing blue and red lights behind us. I knew there was no way we were making it out alive.

Frenchie cut his eyes at me. "Get the fuck out the car, nigga!"

"What? No! Fuck no!"

"You heard what the fuck I said! Get the fuck out the car!"

I glanced over at the dash one more time. Frenchie was pushing his blacked-out Camaro to 170 miles per hour. I knew if I jumped, there would be no way I would've survived, but if I stayed, I'd be better off being dead. Without saying another word, he unlocked the door and tore his eyes away from the road ahead of us to look over at me.

"For the family," I told him.

"For the family," he responded.

I swung the door open and watched the pavement underneath us blur, then jumped. My body skidded off the pavement, and I rolled over and over until I landed in a ditch. I heard the sirens whirring past me as Frenchie kept his foot pressed hard into the gas pedal. I laid there, my adrenaline coursing through my veins. I slowly wiped the water from my eyes. I couldn't tell if they were tears or the rain pouring down.

The second I tried to move, I felt the excruciating pain radiate throughout my entire left side. I could barely move my arm or my leg. I hurt everywhere.

"Ah, fuck!" I groaned as I shifted, trying to keep my arm from aching.

A burning sensation ignited in the back of my eyes, down my spine, and through my veins. I closed my eyes as the pain sheeted my entire body. I knew the longer I laid there, the worse the pain would get. I felt around inside my pocket and exhaled when I was able to pull out my phone and press the last number I'd dialed before my entire night turned to shit. After three rings, my nigga Riot picked up.

"Yo, P. What's good? You and Frenchie straight?"

"N-nah. I ne-need you to come find me."

"Find you? Nigga, what the fuck is going on?"

"Just—fuckin' find me," I mumbled before everything went black.

Chapter One

SAVANNAH MCKINNEY

Beep, beep! Beep, beep!

Red neon lights greeted me as soon as I cracked open my eyes, illuminating my otherwise dark room. My alarm clock continued to blink in my face, 5:00 a.m., until I slammed my hand down on top of it to silence it. As much as I didn't want to, I pried myself away from my warm bedsheets, flipped on my lamp, and headed for my closet.

As soon as I looked at my reflection in the bathroom mirror, butterflies filled my stomach. It wasn't just any day. It was the big day. I was going to receive the FBI medal for Meritorious Achievement for being a part of a huge drug bust in New Mexico, where my team took down Carlos Reyes, one of the biggest drug cartel leaders on this side of the border.

My hands slid down the sharp crease in my navy-blue slacks as I checked myself out in the mirror.

"Hair, check. Lipstick, check. Keys, check. Coffee?" I mumbled to myself.

I scurried into the kitchen adjacent from my bedroom and quickly turned on my Keurig. As soon as the water started to rumble, I realized I didn't have any more K-Cups.

"Fuck," I groaned.

Instead, I grabbed my coat, phone, keys, and purse, and scurried out of the door. Once at work, I grabbed a coffee and a bagel with honey pecan cream cheese. I knew it wasn't the healthiest decision, but I didn't care. I threw my purse down on my desk across from my co-worker and looked at the load of case files piled up on my desk.

"Great. Just great," I mumbled.

"Hey, McKinney. C'mon. The ceremony starts in fifteen minutes," my co-worker Agent Bobby Carter told me.

I nodded. "Coming, Carter."

I took a quick bite into my bagel and washed it down with a splash of hot coffee, then headed down to the auditorium so I wouldn't be late for the ceremony. My unit chief walked up to the podium and smiled at all of us who were seated in the crowd.

"Good morning, everyone. As you all know, today is a very special day. We are here to present the task force team who handled Operation Oracle with the FBI medal for Meritorious Achievement. After nine months of dedicated undercover work, the team was able to bring down Carlos Reyes, who was the head of the Merlindo Cartel in New Mexico."

He paused as cheers and claps filled the room. "Today, we thank Agent Joseph Castillo, Agent Evan Berry, Agent Walter Henson, and last but most certainly not least, Agent Savannah McKinney for their professionalism, their bravery, and their dedication to making the United States a safer place."

Everyone in the room stood to their feet to give us a standing ovation. I was never one to seek the limelight, but recognition for all our hard work did feel good. The four of us walked up to the stage, got our medals, and shook hands with the chief.

"Thank you, sir," I told him.

"Why don't you say a few words? After all, it was your leadership that got the team to victory," he told me.

I reluctantly nodded as one hand gripped the podium while the other rested on the medal. I looked out onto the crowd and squinted my eyes under the bright lights of the stage. I'd never liked public speaking. *'Here goes nothing,'* I thought to myself.

"Um, good morning everyone. I-uh hadn't expected to make any type of speech today, so this will be short. I've never been a woman of too many words, but I would really just like to thank these three men, standing here with me today, for their bravery. I'd also like to thank the ones who aren't here with us today. Two men and one woman lost their lives in the process of trying to make the U.S. a safer place. Let us please take a moment of silence for them."

After a few seconds passed, I started up again. "Going undercover was one of the scariest things I've ever done with my life. You infiltrate someone else's world with the hopes of bringing justice to the forefront in the end, but never know if you'll make it to see it happen. It's exciting. It's nerve wracking. It's our duty to the United States of America. Thank you."

After the ceremony, I went back to my desk in an attempt to finish my bagel with one previous bite in it. As soon as I unlocked my computer to officially get my day started, the chief walked over to my desk.

"McKinney, I'd like to speak with you in my office."

"Right now?"

"Yes, now."

I nodded and huffed at the same time. I had no idea how anyone thought I was going to be able to get any work done if I was never at my desk long enough to do any of it. As soon as I walked into his office, I saw Deputy Director James Shaw in there, and he was already seated. I immediately started to get nervous.

I cleared my throat. "What did you need to speak with me about, sir?"

"Have a seat, Agent McKinney."

I took my seat next to the deputy director and crossed my legs.

"I've asked Deputy Director Shaw here today because I want to talk to you about your performance here at the bureau. But before I start, I'd like to once again congratulate you on your medal today."

"Thank you, sir."

"How long have you been here, McKinney?"

"Um, almost four years."

"And how many undercover task force teams have you been on?"

"Well, the Operation Oracle was my first one, officially."

"And you led that team, correct?"

"Yes, sir. I did."

The room went silent, and I could feel the moistness forming in my underarms. "With all due respect, sir, am I missing something?" I asked hesitantly.

"Do you enjoy what you do for the bureau and for the American people?"

"Yes, I love what I do."

Deputy Director Shaw looked at me. "A position in a special internal affairs unit for a sting operation, Operation November in Chicago, just opened up, and we feel you are the best fit for the job."

"Chicago?"

"Yes, Chicago," he said, handing me a piece of paper with

the job announcement on it. "They need someone like you on their team, Agent McKinney."

"How long is the assignment, sir?"

"There is no time limit, but we want you to get in and out as swiftly and as accurately as possible."

I nodded. "And when would I have to give you my decision?"

"We'd like it by close of business today," the chief chimed in.

I exhaled loudly. "Wow, today? That's short notice."

"The team is in dire need of help from somebody with your level of expertise, Agent McKinney. We need you to decide so we can let the Atlanta region know."

I nodded again. "If I accept, when would I have to report?"

"This Friday."

I sighed inside my head. It was already Tuesday. Short notice was getting shorter and shorter.

"If you accept this, we will take care of your relocation fees. The regional agency in Atlanta will brief you on everything you need to know as soon as your plane lands."

My mind was racing. I didn't know if I was ready to go on another undercover mission. I was one of the younger agents at the bureau and was still trying to find my place in all of it, but if they wanted me, I knew I couldn't turn it down.

"I'll do it."

Chapter Two

SAVANNAH

The moment I stepped off the plane in Atlanta, I was greeted by a fair-skinned woman. I quickly scanned her from head to toe and then shook her outstretched hand.

"Hi, I'm Agent Kelly Adams."

"Agent Savannah McKinney. It's nice to meet you."

"Everyone has talked so highly of you. I'm so glad you accepted the opportunity to come down and be a part of the team."

"Thank you. I'm excited."

"Okay, so once we get your things in the car, I'll take us to the regional office. The briefing starts in thirty minutes, so let's go."

Once we got to the office, Agent Adams led me into the conference room. There were ten people seated around a long, rectangular table and facing the projector.

"Good afternoon, team. I'd like to introduce you to the newest member of our team, Agent Savannah McKinney."

Everyone started clapping, and I smiled. "Hello, everyone. It's great to be here."

The moment I took my seat at the table, someone handed me a manila folder, and the room went dim. Agent Adams stood at the head of the table and started talking. For most of the briefing, I remained quiet and observed everything that was being talked about. My attention was broken when the door opened, and a man walked in.

"Sorry I'm late. It's been hard to get away," he said.

I immediately noticed he was in street clothes.

"Agent McKinney, this is Special Agent-in-Charge Michael Shepard, your co-lead for Operation November," Agent Adams said.

We both looked at each other. I could tell he was stand-offish and the type of guy who didn't do well with sharing the spotlight.

"I take it you don't play well with others," I said, outstretching my hand to him.

"I guess it's true what they say, it takes one to know one, huh?" he replied while firmly shaking my hand.

Everyone in the room laughed. "C'mon, Shep, give the lady a break. It's her first day," one agent shouted out from across the table.

"My first day here, not my first day on the job, remember that. I didn't accept this job to step on anybody's toes. I just want to catch the bad guy like the rest of you," I stated firmly.

The room fell silent, and Agent Adams cleared her throat. "Alright, everyone, let's get back to the reason why we're all here. Shep, take a seat."

He sat beside me and opened his folder. I could smell the hint of cologne radiating off his body. It smelled like a mixture of amber and musk. There was a tattoo of a rose on his left hand and some words scribbled on the side of his neck that I couldn't quite make out.

"As I was saying earlier, Pharaoh Blackwell is one of Chicago's biggest drug kingpins and a gang member. I want you all to take a good look at his face. I want you to know this son of a bitch so good that you see him in your dreams."

I studied the face on the screen. If he hadn't been such a vicious person, I would've thought he was handsome. There was tattoo ink dripping from his throat all the way down to his fingertips. Although he wasn't smiling in any of the photos they had of him on the screen, I could tell there was a perfect set of teeth hiding behind his juicy lips.

"Here's what we know. He's been operating a high traffic and extremely profitable cocaine distribution network. We believe he has suppliers right here in Atlanta, New York City, along the Texas border, and Niagara Falls. Since Blackwell came across our radar five years ago, there have been several hundred kilograms of cocaine transported across the United States. They use tractor-trailers, send packages through the mail, and drug couriers.

Right now, the U.S. Government is at war with drug cartels. They are selling drugs and building criminal enterprises on the backs of the ones they got addicted to the shit in the first place. He's got millions of dollars in illegal narcotics proceeds. Once we get enough information, we'll execute a search warrant and take him down. You can't be sloppy with this, people. I want whatever we can get on him to stick to his ass like glue. Any questions so far?"

I raised my hand. "With all due respect, if you have all of this information on him, why haven't you made an arrest?"

I watched Agent Adams shuffle the paperwork in front of her. "It wasn't for lack of trying, I'll tell you that. We've had some hiccups in the past."

"Like what?"

"Someone in his camp tipping him off. We've also had issues with some obsessive border patrol agents who thought that undercutting us and trying to take his people down at the Texas border would be doing us a favor, but it only makes our job harder."

"We have to hide in plain sight with him and his crew. This isn't like the old days where we could do wiretaps and bugs; not with them. That's a death sentence waiting to happen," Shep said.

"I agree. Agent Shepard has been on this case for about six months now, and through him, we've learned a lot. This guy is no amateur," Agent Adams added.

"So that's what Shepard has been doing? He's infiltrated Blackwell's crew?"

"Yeah, and now it's time to turn it up a notch, and that's where you come in. We can go over the details after this meeting, but for now, just know that my alias is Rico."

"Rico, got it. Continue, I'm listening," I told him.

"Thanks to a tip from a CI, the Chicago police pursued Mr. Frances Blackwell, who just so happens to be Pharaoh's cousin. He's also a notorious member of the BBG."

I quickly scanned my eyes over some of the papers, trying to learn what the acronym stood for. "What is that?"

"The Big Bank Gang," Agent Adams interjected.

"They tried to pull him over for a routine traffic stop, but instead, he fled. Several units pursued the fleeing vehicle down I-90. They believed that Pharaoh was in the car as well, but when the car crashed, police officers tackled the driver who was the only one in the vehicle."

"Where was Pharaoh?"

"We were told that during the high-speed chase with police, he must've escaped. Good news is, Frances is still in custody. We believe he also has direct ties to the drug organization as well."

"And you're sure your CI is trustworthy?"

"I'm sure. DEA caught him selling drugs to an individual working with them. When they searched his motel room, they found a digital scale with powder residue, cocaine, marijuana, and one round of ammunition. He's been convicted of multiple drug offenses, and he's also a lower-ranking member of the BBG. He's the best CI we've had on the case."

"You've had others?"

"Yeah, we have." Agent Adams nodded.

"What happened to them?"

Shepard rolled his eyes. "What do you think?"

I cleared my throat and silently read over Frances's file. He was a felon with two strikes over him already. When they arrested him, he was in possession of a firearm. The police also recovered a small quantity of marijuana, a scale, and a loaded handgun from the trunk of the vehicle. There was no way he was getting out of jail any time soon.

Agent Adams looked at me. "When we catch this son of a bitch, Blackwell, I want to make an example out of his ass. We're going to take him down for everything we can, including operating a criminal enterprise, money laundering, drug conspiracy, the list goes on. When he's convicted, we're seeking a life sentence and a ten-million dollar fine."

I nodded and closed the folder. I had a lot of homework to do before my flight left for Chicago in a few days. A part of me was nervous yet excited. If I could help bring Pharaoh Blackwell down, it would be a notch in my credibility and hopefully a bump in pay.

"Any more questions before we close out, Agent McKinney?"

"Nope, none at all."

"Good, now let's get to work."

Chapter Three

SAVANNAH

Three days later, I was sitting on a plane. "Trip" by Ella Mai was playing in my headphones while I looked out of the window, ignoring all the mandatory safety tips the flight attendants were going over before the plane took off. As soon as the plane ascended into the air, I tilted my head back and started reviewing the notes I'd jotted down about the Blackwell family in my phone. I'd spent the last seventy-two hours learning everything I could about Pharaoh and his cousin Frances. Together, they were a force to be reckoned with.

I connected my phone to the Wi-Fi and started scrolling through my Facebook profile. I accepted a friend request from Jonathan Wilson, an old boyfriend from my early college days at the University of Florida. Out of pure curiosity, I clicked on his name and scrolled through his profile. We'd only been out of college for a few years, and he was already married with a baby on the way. I sighed and locked my phone.

I never did learn how to balance books and boys. I graduated Summa Cum Laude with a bachelor's degree in criminal justice, while Jonathan went off to law school. Shortly after graduation, I was recruited by the FBI and went to Quantico, Virginia for training. From there, I started working at the FBI headquarters in Washington, D.C. Jonathan was my last serious boyfriend. Ever since then, I'd been in a never-ending cycle of "situationships" that were nothing to write home to my mama about. After my last one, I decided to try celibacy. To date, it'd been eleven long months since a man had parted my thighs.

"Attention, passengers, I'm requesting that everyone get back to their seats and put their seat belts on. We've got some bad weather up ahead," the pilot said over the intercom.

I looked out of the window and saw the sky full of frightening, dark clouds. My heart skipped a beat when a flash of lightning tore across the sky, followed by a vibrating rumble of thunder. I turned to see the flight attendant standing near my seat. Even with her crisp navy-blue uniform, stockings, high heels, polished fingernails, neat makeup, and hair, I could tell she was a ball of nerves. I mentally cursed myself for not paying attention on what to do in case of an emergency before the plane took off.

"Everyone, please remain calm. We're just experiencing a bit of turbulence," she announced. "Everything is going to be fine."

As soothing as her words were, her face was anything but. In the blink of an eye, the plane dipped, and my stomach flew up toward my throat as if I was on a rollercoaster. The flight attendant dug her nails into the fabric of the seat beside me, trying her best to stand upright. My eyes darted toward the window, and all I saw was rain pelting at the plane as if we were being shot at.

"Fuck! Fuck, fuck, fuck, fuckkkkkkkk," I groaned while holding onto the seat for dear life.

The plane dropped again, and all I heard were the terrified screams from the people around me. I'd been on an airplane a million times and not once did I think my life would end like that. The second I locked eyes with the flight attendant, I knew it was over for us all.

"Take my hand," I told her as calmly as I could.

The faster the plane dipped toward the ground, the more screams and sheer panic I heard. She grabbed my hand and strapped herself into the vacant seat beside me.

"This is my first flight since getting out of training. I—I don't know what to do," she cried.

My chest rattled with fear as the ride got bumpier. The lower we got to the ground, the harder the rain came down, rattling the plane as if it was a plastic toy. We'd gone from 35,000 feet in the air to practically nosediving right back into God's green earth. People were screaming and praying to whatever God they served, and babies were crying. Panic coursed through my blood. It was almost over. I closed my eyes and gave the flight attendant's hand a tight squeeze.

"I'm so fucking scared," she cried. "I don't wanna die."

Tears streamed down my face. I couldn't even bear to look at her. I'd already seen too much, and I didn't want to see death coming for me. The second the plane slammed into the ground, over half of the plane exploded in flames, and the right wing tore off like a piece of loose-leaf paper.

I opened my eyes to see flames flickering all around me. The heat from the flames felt like hell on earth. I was completely drenched in jet fuel, but I was still breathing. I was alive. The hard rain and the thick smoke from the crash made it almost impossible to see and breathe. I looked over at the flight attendant whose hand was still gripped to mine.

"We...We made it," I whispered to her while coughing.

When I didn't hear a response, I tried to check her pulse, but I couldn't find one. I undid my seat belt and tried my best to dance around the flames to find an exit.

"We have to jump," a man told me. "It's the only way."

I looked at him, and he outstretched his hand to me. I

inhaled, closed my eyes, and jumped. The second we hit the ground, everything went black.

PHARAOH

I woke up in the hospital feeling like I'd been hit by a Mack truck. It took me a second to even realize how I'd gotten there. I immediately checked my wrists for handcuffs and took a sigh of relief when I didn't see any. My eyes darted from the left side of the room to the right. To the left of me were a pair of crutches.

"Great, you're awake," the nurse said as she walked over to me.

I eyed her closely as she started inserting things into my IV. "What are you doing? What are you giving me?"

"Relax, Mr. Blackwell. It's just fluids. This is how we've been keeping you hydrated."

"How long have I been in here?"

"Only a couple of days. Do you remember how you got here?"

I paused for a second, trying to figure out how much of the truth I wanted to tell her. "I remember it was raining heavy… and I was in the car. That's it."

"Yes, and your car hydroplaned, and you were ejected. You fractured your left wrist and right ankle."

"I guess that's what the crutches are for, huh?"

She chuckled. "Exactly."

"When am I going to be cleared to leave? I can't stay here," I told her while trying to remove the tubes from my arm.

"Whoa, settle down. You're not going anywhere yet. If you try to leave before you're ready, you'll only do yourself more harm than good," she warned.

I rolled my eyes. "Stop with the fluids and shit. I'm good. I don't need it."

She sighed. "Well, would you like a real meal?"

"I don't like hospitals, and I damn sure don't like hospital food, so I'll pass," I grumbled.

"Suit yourself. I'll be in to check on you in a little bit," she said and turned to leave the room.

"Hold up a second. Did I have a phone on me when I came in here?"

She pointed. "All your belongings are over there in the chair by the window."

I shot her a nod. "Thanks."

As soon as the door closed, I swung my legs over the bed and gently got up, making sure not to apply too much pressure to my right ankle. I limped over to my jeans and fished my phone out of my pocket. My battery was on less than five percent, and I had over thirty missed calls.

"Niggas probably think I'm dead," I mumbled.

With the limited battery life I had left, I called Riot to see what had been going on since I'd been in the hospital. I had no idea what'd happened to Frenchie, but I knew the police were going to be on my ass.

"Pharaoh, nigga! What the fuck! I thought your ass was fuckin' dead, my nigga! What's good?" Riot answered.

"Yo, I'm still in the hospital, and my phone and shit is about to die. I need you to go by my spot, get me some clean clothes and a charger, and get over here as soon as you can."

"They lettin' you out today?"

"No, but fuck that shit. I'm leavin' anyway. What they gon' do to stop me?"

"Aight, bet. Just chill out for a second, nigga. I got you."

I let out a silent sigh of relief. "Aight," I told him and hung up.

The moment I started inching back over to the bed, my door opened. My head swung up to see a girl standing there with a confused look on her face.

"Can I help you?" I asked, leaning against the bed.

"I take it this isn't my room, huh?" she asked.

"Nah, it definitely ain't."

She lowered her eyes. "I'm sorry... I haven't been myself lately. The doctors want me to walk around, and every time I do, I end up somewhere I'm not supposed to be."

"It's cool."

"Sorry, again."

"I said it's cool; stop apologizing, girl."

She nodded. "Right, okay, well. I'll see you around... or not."

"Hold up. What's your name?" I asked her.

"Savannah... Although I think I recall the people here referring to me as Jane Doe in room 221A."

"Jane Doe, huh? I like Savannah better."

She smirked. "Yeah, I think I do, too."

"Take care of yourself, Savannah."

"Thank you, you too...?"

"Ro," I told her.

"Got it."

I watched her leave until I couldn't see her anymore, then got back in the bed. I tried to watch TV to pass the time, but every time I found myself drifting off into random thought, Savannah's face popped into my head. There was another knock on the door, and Riot entered.

"What up, nigga? How you feelin'?" he asked as he dapped me up.

"I'm good. Nothin' but a few scrapes and bruises here and there."

"They got you on crutches, nigga?"

"I guess. I ain't used them yet. They said I fractured my wrist and my ankle."

"Yo, like, I ain't gon' front, you had a nigga worried. What the fuck really happened, nigga?"

"Close the door," I told him.

Once Riot closed the door, he came over and sat in the chair across from me. "Real talk, all I remember is Frenchie tellin' me to get the fuck out of the car while his ass was doing a thousand down the highway."

"Hold up. You jumped out of a movin' car, my nigga?"

"Yeah. We were bein' chased by the cops. It was either jail or death, and you already know which one I'm choosin'."

"All day, every day," he said, dapping me up again. "But for real, nigga, I can't believe you survived that shit. Niggas said French had to have been pushing the gas all the way down into the floorboards."

I shrugged. "You know me: half man, half amazing."

"Yeah, fuck all that amazing shit, nigga, you just lucky."

"That too."

"When you get out of here?"

"Today. I don't give a fuck what they say. I got shit to do.

How's French? What's going on with that? Did he make it out?"

Riot lowered his head. "Nah, man."

"Is he… Is he dead?"

"Nah, they caught him."

"What?"

"Yeah, nigga wrecked his Camaro and everything. He's locked up. Elite called up to the jail the night it happened, and they told her they found all types of shit on him."

"Man, fuck!" I yelled.

"Yeah, it's not lookin' good for my nigga."

I leaned my head back against the pillow. I'd escaped the law again, but at the expense of my cousin. We'd been living lives filled with money, fast cars, and even faster women, but it seemed as if we were about to lose it all.

"Fuck!"

"But you already know we gon' do whatever we gotta do to get his ass back home, so don't even worry about it."

"I'm not worried, nigga. I'm angry."

"Bet you I can make yo' ass laugh though."

I looked at him with a *"nigga, what crazy shit is about to come out of your mouth now"* face, and he laughed.

"So, check this shit out right. I meet this bitch at the club a few nights ago, get her number and shit. I mean, I had to. She had on this tight ass dress with her ass fallin' out the bottom. It was like God just put her in front of me for a reason.

Anyway, so we textin' and shit, she flirtin' and tryin' to get to know a nigga, and I'm like yeah, I'm not about all that. What that mouth do, you know? So, she finally drop a pin for a nigga, and I head over to the crib. She opens the door with nothin' on but a smile, my nigga. So, you know me, I'm like, damn, this bitch 'bout to make the genie come out the bottle on sight. I like this!

So we get to fuckin' around. She on top, ridin' my shit like a brand-new Harley, you feel me? I'm like okay, bitch, I might have to save your number for real. She doin' all this moanin' and screamin' and shit while I'm smackin' her ass. I turn her over to start givin' her some back shots, and I'm like aww shit, a nigga about to nut, so I pull out.

At first, I was like I'ma nut on this bitch ass, but then I was like nah, why make a mess? So she gets on her knees and start givin' me top and shit and then we hear keys in the door. She stopped suckin' and started talkin' about some, 'what do I do?' I'm like 'bitch, you got a roommate or somethin'?' She's like 'no, it's my husband.' I said 'well, get on your feet!' She talkin' 'bout some 'but I'm not done yet.' I was like 'bitch, you right,' and stuck my dick right back in her mouth and bust all in that shit."

"Nigga, you wild as a bitch." I laughed.

"Nigga, me? She was talkin' 'bout spending forever with a nigga and had a whole husband! These bitches sheisty. That's why I fuck 'em and send 'em on they merry fuckin' way. You can't trust these hoes."

"Nah, you definitely can't."

"I ain't wanna have to pull up on a nigga all because his wife was a whore, but fuck that nigga. He the real sucka for marrying her anyway." He shrugged.

I shook my head when there was a knock on the door. We both turned our attention to it and watched the nurse walk in.

"I'm back with your pain medicine."

"Nah, you can keep it. I don't want it."

"Shit, if he don't want it, I'll take it," Riot interjected.

I cut my eyes at him. "I'm good. As soon as I get dressed, I'm leavin'."

"Mr. Blackwell, I already told you—"

"I know what you said, but you're not listening to what I'm saying. As soon as I get dressed, I'm leaving here today."

"Are you sure you at least don't want to take the medicine with you?"

"I'll take it, but I'm not gon' use it."

"Trust me, if you leave here now in your condition without this medication, you're gonna wish you didn't."

She left the pills in a small cup beside my bed and turned her back to me. "I'll be back with your discharge papers."

"Damn, nigga. That was cold," Riot told me.

"I told you I wasn't stayin'. What I look like lounging around in a hospital bed when my blood is sittin' in a fuckin' cell? I got shit to handle."

Riot stood to his feet and nodded. "I'ma let you get dressed and shit. I'll be in the car."

He walked over and grabbed the two pills out of the cup and swallowed them. "I hope you don't mind."

"Nigga, get out! I'll be down in a minute."

"Bet. Trust me, when French come home and you feelin' up to it, we gon' celebrate, believe that. Everything gon' be straight soon enough."

Chapter Four

PHARAOH

Just before I walked out of the hospital doors, I caught a glimpse of Savannah again. She was downstairs, in the cafeteria, holding a green apple in her hand. She must've felt me looking at her because she looked dead at me and smiled.

"You again."

I smiled. "Yeah, what's up?"

"You gettin' out of here?"

"Yeah, I am. It's… Savannah, right?"

"That's what my bracelet says," she said, holding up her left wrist.

I nodded with a smile. "You know your room number now?" I asked, partially joking, partially serious.

She scratched the side of her head and giggled. "Again, I am so sorry about that."

"Nah, you good. What is it though?"

"What is what?"

"Your room number."

"Room 221A."

"Cool, just checking."

"Well, take care of yourself… Ro?"

"Yeah, Ro."

The two of us stood awkwardly in each other's presence for a few seconds before I turned around on my crutches and started going the other way. She went back to whatever it was she was doing, and I caught eyes with the associate standing behind the counter in the gift shop to my right. There were fresh bouquets of flowers, stuffed animals, cards, and balloons inside. I hobbled inside and walked up to the counter.

"Can I help you, sir?"

"Uh, yeah... I want something delivered to room 221A."

"No problem. What would you like? We have candy, stuffed animals—"

"Yeah, I can see all that. Shit, I don't know... If you was in the hospital, what would you want someone to bring you?"

"I've always been a sucker for flowers," she told me.

"Flowers, huh?"

"Yeah; every woman loves a fresh bouquet of flowers."

"I don't know about all that, but I'll take your word for it," I told her.

"Great. What would you like? Roses?"

"Roses is fine. How much?"

"That'll be fifty-two dollars even."

I reached into my wallet and pulled out a crisp one-hundred-dollar bill and laid it on the counter.

"I'm sorry, sir, but I don't think I have enough money to give you back your change."

"I'm not worried about change. Keep it. Just make sure she gets the flowers."

"What do you want the card to say?"

"What card?"

"For the flowers... There's always a notecard attached so the person knows who they are from."

I rested my weight on my good ankle and paused for a few seconds. I had never sent a female a bouquet of flowers in my life. It just wasn't my style, so I had no idea what to say.

"Just write, 'Get better. Ro'."

Her face frowned, and she cleared her throat. "How about, Get well soon. Love, Ro."

"Take that love shit out, and we good," I told her.

"Okay. I'll have these personally delivered within the next few minutes. Thank you, and I hope you get well soon as well," she told me.

"Yeah, thanks."

SAVANNAH

A few days after the crash, I woke up in a hospital bed with nothing but a fractured collarbone, a few cuts on my arms, and the loss of my short-term memory. A part of me was thankful I didn't remember much about the crash or anything within a week before it. I'd been walking around like a zombie, trying to figure out what had happened in my life that I'd forgotten, but to no avail.

The nurses and doctors all told me how lucky I was to have been alive. Out of the 130 people on the flight, only me and three other people survived. Everyone else died during the crash, or shortly after, from burns, injuries, or excessive smoke inhalation. Every time I flipped on the TV, the local stations were talking about the crash, but I was so numb to it all that I couldn't even cry about it.

"How are you feeling today, Savannah?" the nurse asked as she entered the room.

"Thankful." I shrugged.

"I have a surprise for you."

"What is it?"

She stepped outside and came back in with a large, beautiful bouquet of fresh red roses. "These are for you."

"You got me flowers?" I asked.

"These are definitely not from me, sweetie. Why don't you read the card to see who they're from?"

I grabbed the card and scanned it from left to right. "Get well soon, Ro."

"I knew it was a man who sent you these! Who's the lucky guy?"

"There is no lucky guy... He's... I don't know who he is. I just met him here."

"He must be smitten with you already to have sent you flowers."

"No, I think he was just being nice," I told her.

"Whatever you say, sweetie. I'll be back in with your pain medication shortly. Have you remembered anything else from the crash or the days leading up to it?"

"Nope, not yet." I sighed.

"Well, at least you're still here. That's the luck of the draw if you ask me."

"Everybody keeps telling me that, that I'm lucky to be alive, but I don't feel lucky at all. I feel empty like there's this big ass hole sitting in the middle of my head that air just passes through, and there's nothing there to fill it."

She walked over to me and rested her hand on my shoulder. "Look, I've been a nurse for over twenty years. I've seen more than your eyes could even possibly imagine. There's a lot that comes with surviving something like this, Savannah. Nobody comes out of something like that without some sort of injury, whether its external or internal."

"How am I supposed to cope with something I can't even remember?" I asked as tears filled my eyes. "God! This is so frustrating!"

"You take each day as it comes, that's all you can do. It'll all work itself out in due time."

I nodded while wiping the dampened corners of my eyes and looked up when I heard a knock on the door.

"McKinney, how are you?" the chief asked, followed by a woman.

"I'm still here, sir."

He reached out his hand to shake mine. "You remember Agent Adams, right?"

I looked in her eyes, and as much as I wanted to please everyone in the room, I shook my head. I had no idea who she was. "No, sir. The doctors said that all the smoke inhalation from the crash caused me to lose significant oxygen to my brain, which temporarily took away my short-term memory."

"So you don't remember anything?" he asked.

"Not the crash and anything at least a few days before it."

"So you don't remember coming to Atlanta... or anything?" she added.

I huffed, unsure as to why she would ask me the same question I'd just answered. "The last thing I remember was getting my award; after that, it's all one big blur."

The two of them shot knowing looks at each other and then looked at the nurse. "Can we get a few minutes alone with her, please?" the chief asked.

"Of course. I'll be down the hall if you need me. Just buzz the nurses' station," she said and left the room.

The chief walked over and sat at the foot of my hospital bed, while Agent Adams stood a few feet away.

"How are you really doing, Savannah? Physically, you look fine, but I mean, mentally…"

I shrugged. "I've been walking around with this guilt on my chest for something that I don't even remember… Like, why am I still here? Why didn't I die with everyone else?"

"What you're feeling is normal. You went through a terrifying experience that will probably alter the way you think, breathe, act, and talk for the rest of your life. There's nothing wrong with feeling confused or even guilty," he told me.

I nodded. "Thanks, Chief."

"Do you feel up to being briefed on Operation November again really quickly?" Agent Adams asked.

I nodded. "Yes, of course."

She walked closer to us and pulled up a chair to my bedside. "We currently have Frances Blackwell in custody. We had good intel that his cousin, who we really want, was with him, but when Blackwell was finally apprehended, he was alone."

"And you can't get Frances to talk?" I asked.

"Not a word, but that's to be expected. He's the leader of a gang here in Chicago. He's not going to snitch. That would be going against everything he stands for."

"It's hard to tell which one of them is the true enforcer. They both have iron fists," the chief added.

"What charges are you holding Frances Blackwell on?"

"Right now, Chicago PD has him on first-degree murder of LaDavius Millwood. We believe he was given the green light to murder Millwood over a gang war that was taking place inside the prison. As soon as Millwood was released, he was killed less than twelve hours later."

My eyes widened. "Wow."

"Yeah, but don't get it twisted. His gang isn't just your average neighborhood gang. They are a subset of the Bloods, and they don't fuck around," the chief intervened.

"So you want both Blackwell guys to go down for gang affiliated murders?"

"No, we want Frances for the murder and his cousin for drug trafficking and distribution of crack cocaine, marijuana, and other illicit narcotics such as heroin and pills."

Agent Adams nodded. "This guy is like the jack of all trades when it comes to drug dealing."

"Is the DEA in on this?"

"Yes," they said in unison.

"So why are we tailing Frances's cousin? It sounds like we got the guy we need for the gang murders. Why not let DEA handle the rest?"

The chief sighed. "To be honest, I think this is more than they can handle. These drugs are flooding the streets of Chicago, and it's going to take more than a few DEA agents to put an end to it. Whether they think so or not, they need us to stay on."

I nodded. "Tell me more about Frances's cousin."

"We know that millions of dollars in drug money are being transported each week from his drug markets around the U.S. and surrounding borders, to stash houses here in Chicago. We just don't quite know where yet."

"So you think this guy is just sitting on a pile of money somewhere?"

"No. We believe he's laundering it through some business. I just don't know what kind yet. It's nothing big like a club or a regular blue-collar business, but it's something that's smart enough to keep him flying just under our radar."

"How'd you find out about him in the first place?"

"Frances's moves led us right to him. At first, we had no interest in his cousin, but when we saw that he's taking direct control of the money... he became another person of interest on our corkboard."

I shifted in the bed while clasping my hands together. "What do you need me to do?"

"We already have Agent Michael Shepard undercover inside the gang. We need you to infiltrate his business. Find out as much as you can about him. Where are his stash houses located? How is he bringing drugs into the city? Who is his connect? If we can get any of those answers, we can lock him away for good," Agent Adams told me.

"He sounds like a straight up monster. Do you have a photo of him?"

She shook her head. "No, I don't have one with me, but he is a monster, and he needs to be put behind bars for life. We want to bring Blackwell in on a laundry list of charges that include drug trafficking, gang affiliated-related killings, and money laundering. The more we have that can stick to him, the less chances he has of getting away."

"I'm ready to be the one to do it as soon as they let me out of here. Putting him behind bars will be the pinnacle of my career."

"This is going to be the most dangerous job you've ever done, but you're not ready to come back just yet," the chief said while patting my hand.

"What do you mean? I feel okay."

"Can you remember what you ate for breakfast yesterday?"

I paused. "I had a-a um..."

He sighed and patted my shoulder. "Memory loss can be tricky. It can come back all at once, come back in waves, or not at all."

"But it's short-term. I still remember my training. I still remember my oath. I remember most things, just not everything."

"Savannah, we talked to your doctor before we came to see you. He said he doesn't quite know where you fall on the spectrum just yet. So until then, we've got you set up in an apartment downtown. You go there, recuperate to the fullest, make all your doctor appointments and therapy sessions to get you back as good as new, and then you're on again."

Although it wasn't the news I wanted to hear, I accepted it. At least they still wanted me on the job and weren't sending me on a plane back home to D.C. "Thank you, sir."

"No, thank you. Take care of yourself. I'll be in touch."

Chapter Five

SAVANNAH

I was released from the hospital a few days later and went to the apartment that the agency had set up for me. They spared no expense. There were floor-to-ceiling windows in the kitchen, living room, and bedroom that overlooked the city. The entire place came pre-furnished and had stainless steel appliances. It put my shoebox apartment in Northeast D.C. to shame.

I put my limited belongings down on the kitchen countertop and admired the view. All my luggage had been burned in the plane crash, along with my phone and anything else I had on me. All I had was the sweat suit on my back from the hospital and an American Express card, courtesy of the U.S. Government to purchase myself some new clothing, a new phone, food, and toiletries.

As soon as my Uber dropped me off downtown, I started shopping. Within the first hour, I'd racked up almost a thousand dollars in debt on that AMEX. I walked out of the store with bags in both hands when I ran into a man.

"Oh shit, my fault," he said as he bent down to pick up the bags that'd flown out of my hands.

I looked up at him, and my forehead scrunched up. "You."

"You," he repeated.

"It's Ro, right?"

"Yeah, well Pharaoh."

"That's a nice name. How are you?"

"Healing. You?"

I nodded. "Same. I'm actually trying to find a place to get my hair done; being in the hospital left me with a serious case of bed head."

"Oh, you not from here?"

"No, I'm actually from the east coast."

"Word. I should've known."

"What's that supposed to mean?" I asked.

"Nothin'. I can just tell your swag is a little different. I didn't mean to offend you."

"You didn't…"

"So, uh… You said you were tryin' to get your hair done, right? I might know a spot that's not too far from here."

"Oh yeah? What's it called?"

"Elite Hair. My cousin girl owns the shop over on the southside."

"Thanks, I'll uh… I'll check it out. What's the address?"

"I'm actually headed over that way if you wanted to catch a ride," he offered.

I stopped to look at him for a moment. He was a gorgeous man. Too gorgeous to be faithful. He had a smile like a loaded gun; one flash, and I'd be dead. He had tattoos that dripped from the back of his head all the way down to his hands. Although he was fully clothed, I could tell he had a rock-hard body.

"So... Is that a yes or...?"

"I'm sorry," I said, snapping out of my daze. "But um, as flattered as I am, I don't get in the car with strangers unless I'm paying them for a ride."

"Good answer."

"Was that some sort of test?"

"Yeah, it kinda was."

I cocked my head to the side. "So... did I pass?"

"Yes, you did." He nodded.

"Mm hmm, so what's the address?"

"I'll text it to you," he said.

I chuckled. "Another test, huh?"

He laughed. "I'm just kidding with you. It's 871 South State Street."

"Thanks. I'll check it out."

I turned to walk away and then stopped. "Oh, and um, thank you... for the flowers."

He smirked. "I was beginning to think you either never got them, or you just don't fuck with flowers."

"What girl doesn't like flowers?"

He shrugged. "I don't know, but you're welcome though."

"What made you wanna do something nice like that? You barely know me."

He shrugged again. "Damn, a nigga can't do nothin' nice nowadays without being questioned, huh?"

"I'm sorry. I was just curious. I didn't mean to offend you."

"I'm not offended, trust me. But nah, you seemed like you were going through it, so I thought it was the least I could do."

"Well, thank you."

"You welcome... You know that's not even my style, right?"

"What?"

"That flower shit. I've never sent a female any type of flower in my life."

"Then what do you do?" I asked.

"This," he said, pulling out his wallet. "Consider this your hood get well soon bouquet."

He outstretched his hand to give me two crisp one-hundred-dollar bills, and I scrunched up my nose. "Um... I know my hair may be a little crazy, but I don't think it'll cost two franklins."

"I'm never sure of how much it costs to get y'all shit done. Take it, enjoy it."

"You wouldn't be trying to buy me, would you?"

"Nah, never that. I would never pay for something I could get for free."

I scoffed. "Get for free from who?"

He shook his head. "Nah, I didn't mean it like that. I just meant... you know what? Never mind. Let me just stop while I'm ahead."

"Yeah, I think you should too."

"So you gon' take the money or leave me standin' here holdin' it, lookin' crazy?"

I took the money from him and put it in my pocket. "Only because something tells me this money is nothing to you, and Mama ain't raise no fool."

"I'll see you around."

"Maybe you will, maybe you won't," I told him.

From the second Ro left my presence, my body wouldn't stop tingling. Just his conversation alone had sparked something inside me. At the end of the day, he was a stranger to me. He was dark, and mysterious, but there was a light about him that I attached to for some reason. He stayed on my mind from the Uber ride back to my apartment and then all the way to the salon on the southside.

The bells on the handle jingled as soon as I opened the door to the salon. "Welcome to Elite Hair, can I help you?" the receptionist asked.

"Yes, um... I just need to get a wash and a flatiron."

"Any stylist in particular?"

"No. I'm new here, so I don't know anyone. Who's your best one?" I asked.

"The best would be Elite. She's the owner, but she's not here today."

"You can send her to me, Nique. I'll take good care of her," a female stylist said from the shampoo area.

"Okay, thank you."

I walked toward the back of the salon and admired the modern décor. Each shampoo bowl had plush cushioned seats, and each individual station had their own full-length mirror in front of it. There were chandeliers hanging from the ceiling, and the maple hardwood floor shined as if it was brand new.

"Welcome to Elite Hair, I'm Toya. What's your name?"

"I'm Savannah."

"Nice to meet you, Savannah. Have a seat, and let's see what we workin' with here."

"Okay, but I'm just warning you, it's not tamed. I've been

in the hospital with no hair products and cheap ass combs, so you can do the math."

"I feel you. Don't worry; we gon' take good care of you here."

I closed my eyes as the warm water flowed all over my scalp. As much as I could've fallen asleep, all the chatter around me was keeping me too entertained.

"Girl, did you hear about Elite's man getting locked up?" another stylist asked Toya.

"Yeah, that's why she ain't been here."

"That's so fucked up, and she just had that new baby, too. This is terrible timing."

"Who you tellin'? But hey, that's what you sign up for when you fuck with a nigga in the BBG," Toya told her.

"Hell yeah. I be trying to tell my little fast ass sister about runnin' around behind one of those dumb ass boys at her school. He is so pressed to be down with the BBG, and she is so pressed to be his. It's disgusting."

"Yeah, but we all had our little bad boy fetish phase."

"Yeah, until you find out he ain't shit after you done had two kids with him and let 'em stick his dick all in your ass and shit."

"Hold up, bitch, what the fuck are you on?" Toya laughed.

"I'm just sayin', girl, you gotta have real skill and be willin' to live life on the edge if you wanna be with a BBG nigga. They ain't your average niggas."

"Especially not that fine ass fuckin' Pharaoh," Toya said.

"Bitch, who you tellin'? Your pussy gotta be top of the line for that nigga. Like, you gotta be able to bring Jesus to his knees to keep a nigga like that."

"Is he really that great?" I asked, while mentally rolling my eyes.

I knew my instincts were right. Pharaoh's ass was too fine to be good news, and they were about to prove me right without even knowing it.

"Is he? Girl, listen, either you've been livin' under a rock or your ass ain't from here, because everybody and they mama, they grandmama, and they aunties too, know who Pharaoh is."

"Yeah, I'm actually not from here."

"Where you from?"

"D.C by way of Florida."

"See, yup, that explains it. Okay, so let me break it down for you. Pharaoh and his crew are the sexiest niggas in the city," Toya explained.

"Don't forget they the biggest ballers in the city, too," the other stylist added.

"Right. Nobody fucks with him or his crew."

"Unless they want a death sentence."

"Okay!" Toya said, slapping her hand. "But yeah, to get with some of the lower ranking niggas don't take nothin' but a fat ass and a pretty smile, but to get with the top dogs like Riot or Frenchie, you gotta bring more to the table, and to get with Pharaoh, bitch, you've got to have the pussy skills of an acrobatic stripper."

"What? Is it really that serious? What do you even mean by that?" I chuckled.

"Keisha, tell her what I mean."

Toya sat me up so that I could turn my attention to Keisha, who was standing at the wash bowl beside me, dying some weave. I watched the way she popped the gum in her mouth as she looked me up and down.

"I need a nigga who gone swipe the visa, the AMEX, shit, the green dot card, whatever! It needs to be on demand! Pharaoh got that!"

"I heard he got that on demand dick, too," Toya said, oozing with lust.

I shrugged. "He's a rich hood celebrity, so what? He's still just a guy, right?"

"You don't get it."

"What's there not to get? He's like the typical hood prodigy. Aren't niggas like him like a dime a dozen?"

They both blew hot air out of their mouths and shook their heads. "It's a known fact that every nigga in BBG got BDE."

"BDE?" I asked.

"Big dick energy, girl. Every bitch need a nigga with that, you feel me? Now, Pharaoh... I mean, one look at the nigga and you'll be cleaning up panty soup in your good drawers, you know?"

"I second that shit," Keisha added.

They both burst out laughing as another stylist walked over and patted me on the shoulder. "Don't mind these two. You know what they say: you can take the girls out the hood, but you can't take the hood out the girls."

"Girl, look the fuck around you! We still in the hood!" Keisha told her and burst out laughing again.

"What y'all back here talkin' about anyway?"

"Trying to explain to the new girl here that she needs to go on and try her luck with the BBG while she's in town."

"BBG? Bitch, are you crazy? Listen to me. Don't listen to nothin' these crazy broads are tellin' you," she warned me.

"C'mon, Jaz. What's wrong with BBG?"

"Girl, please! I'm not fuckin' with none of them crazy ass niggas. Shit, some of 'em fine and all, but the dick ain't worth my life. I heard how them niggas get down."

"Shit, all I know is closed legs don't get fed," Keisha told her.

Toya nodded. "And never will."

I SPENT THE next hour and a half drowning in conversation after conversation about Pharaoh. As annoying as it was, Toya brought my hair back to life and only charged me one-hundred dollars. I felt like a new woman walking out of the salon. I walked down to the corner and started waiting for my Uber when I heard someone call my name.

"Two times in one day for the second time in a row? I'm starting to think you're stalking me," I told Pharaoh as soon as he got close enough to hear me.

"Crazy, right?"

"So I guess you really weren't lying about coming on this side of town, now were you?"

"Nah, that was the truth. Your hair looks nice."

"Thank you. She did a really good job. Thanks for the recommendation."

"No problem."

"You were quite the hot topic in the hair salon you sent me to, but something tells me you already knew that," I told him.

"Oh, really?"

"Yeah, you were."

"Nah, I didn't know that. What'd they say about me?"

"Mmm, wouldn't you like to know." I chuckled.

"Yeah, I would. How about you tell me over lunch."

"Lunch?"

"Oh, my fault. You one of those girls who don't eat?"

"Definitely not," I said, while rolling my eyes.

"Good, then let's go."

"Wait, let me just get this straight. First you pay for my hair, then you ask me out to eat... Hmm..."

"What? You think I'm doing too much?"

"I didn't say that."

"Then what is it?"

"It's nothing. It's just... nice, I guess."

His forehead creased. "Nice, you guess?"

"Yeah."

"Aight, I'll take that... *I guess*."

I smiled. "Shut up... Where are we even going?"

"Right down the street. There's this place called Chicago's Chicken and Waffles. They have the best soul food in the city as far as soul food is concerned."

"Okay. You were on point with the hair salon, so I trust you know good food when you taste it."

"Yeah, and you will too."

Once we were seated and our orders had been placed, I looked up at him. "Question."

"Shoot," he said.

"What landed you in the hospital?"

"Long story."

"Well, lucky for you my food isn't here yet, so I've got time."

He shifted in his seat and shook his head. "I was in a car accident. There was a bad storm and shit just went left. What about you?"

"Did you hear about the plane that crashed recently?"

"Nah, I think I must've missed that... You were on it?"

"Yeah, I was... And as a result of it, I've lost my short-term memory. I don't remember anything from the crash or from a few days before. Doctors say it's a fifty/fifty chance if I get it back or not, but I'll just have to wait it out and see. Somedays, I wish I could remember; other days, I pray the memories never return."

"It may be a good thing."

"What do you mean?" I asked.

"Sometimes memories are the worst form of torture. Look at it as a blessing. You get to rewrite a part of life and start fresh, and you're in a new city, too? You can be anybody you want."

"Is that what you would do if you were me?"

"I don't know... I can't really picture my life as anything other than what it is right now," he admitted.

"I bet. You know, with all your fans flocking around the city and all, who wouldn't wanna be you."

He rolled his eyes. "There you go with that shit again. You still ain't gon' tell me what they said?"

"Eh, something about you being a baller and a bad ass, and in order for any woman to get with you, she'd have to be extra, completely top of the line special. To be completely honest, the fandom was nauseating."

He chuckled. "Damn, all that?"

"Yeah."

"They're right though."

"About what?"

"A woman would have to be extra, completely top of the line special to be mine."

"Oh, right. You just pay for the extra not special ones to get their hair done, huh?" I chuckled.

The waitress brought over our food, and once she left, he looked at me. "You got a smart-ass mouth, Savannah."

I smirked. "So I've been told. Oh, before I forget, here you go," I said, handing him the one-hundred-dollar bill back that I didn't spend.

"What's this for?"

"My hair... It didn't cost the whole two hundred, so I'm being a good Samaritan and giving you back your change."

"Keep that shit, Savannah. I'm not worried about that."

I watched him press a napkin against his lips with a surprised look on my face.

"What?" he asked.

"A hood nigga with couth. Now that's rare..." I mumbled.
"You not ready for this. A nigga like me can really show you something."
"Mm hmm. I won't lie; after all that talk they did about you in the shop, I tried to look you up on social media and couldn't find a trace of you."
"Yeah, I don't do none of that social shit."

"Excuse me? Exactly how old are you?"

"I'm twenty-five."

"You say that like it's old? You're only a year older than me."

"Is that right?"

Before I could respond, he pulled his phone out of his pocket and got up. "I'll be back."

He walked out of the restaurant while I continued to eat my food. As much as I didn't want to admit it, he'd picked a good place to eat. Pharaoh came back over to the table five minutes later and stood over me.

"Hey, um, I gotta go."

"Is everything okay?"

"Yeah. Give me your phone."

"For what?"

"I'm gon' put my number in it."

"What have I done to deserve such a high honor?" I asked with a hint of sarcasm in my voice.

"Consider yourself extra, completely top of the line special," he said, followed by a smile.

I handed him my phone and watched him put his number in. He put the money on the table to pay for lunch and handed me back my phone.

"Should I expect to hear from you?"

"Yeah, maybe... Thanks for lunch... and the hair... and the flowers."

"You welcome. Enjoy the rest of your day, Savannah."

PHARAOH

A part of me felt bad for leaving Savannah inside the restaurant how I did, but I had business to handle. Frenchie had been released from jail due to lack of evidence, and we were going to throw him a welcome home party he'd never forget.

I pulled up to Frenchie's house and got out. A few seconds after ringing the doorbell, his daughter Imani answered.

"Hi, Uncle P."

"Hey, princess. Where's your daddy at?"

"In the room with Mommy. I'll go get him."

I walked inside and closed the door behind me, then sat on the couch next to Paxton's swing. He was French's newborn son. I waited for ten minutes before French came downstairs with no shirt on and a pair of basketball shorts.

"What up, fam?" he asked, walking over to dap me up.

We pulled each other into a hug, and he walked over and picked up his son from the swing and sat beside me on the couch.

"How you feelin'? You good, nigga?" I asked.

"Yeah, I'm straight. That ain't the first time I been behind bars, and it probably won't be my last." He shrugged. "How you feelin'? Riot told me they tried to keep you in the hospital and you left anyway."

"Hell yeah. What I look like sittin' in the hospital when my family is behind bars. What the fuck even happened after I jumped out?"

He shook his head. "Man, they found my gun on me and yours, some drugs I had on me, and took my ass in. They ain't waste no time once I got there. They wanted to know about the drugs, BBG, shit, even you."

"I fuckin' knew they were gon' try and flip you."

"Yeah, but you know me. I wasn't worried about none of that shit. The only thing that had me a lil' fucked up was when they brought up that Millwood nigga shit. They tryna pin it on me just because after he got out of jail, he got killed. How the fuck is that my fault?"

I looked at him and leaned in closer. "You talkin' about the nigga you and Riot hit?"

"Yeah, that punk ass bitch."

"How the fuck they even know about that shit?"

He shrugged. "I don't fuckin' know, nigga. I swear to God we better not have no snitch amongst us. That's the only way I can even see some shit gettin' out like that."

"Who all knows besides you, me, and Riot?" I asked.

"Junie, Gino… oh, and Rico."

"You see, that's too many fuckin' niggas right there. Look, I don't have time for this shit. We did what we had to do to make sure the money kept flowin' in. If a nigga had to lose his life so we can continue to eat, then that's fine; I don't give a fuck. I just don't need the fuckin' police on my dick."

"Nah, I feel you, nigga. Trust and believe, I got both eyes wide open on all these niggas."

"Good."

"The only reason they let me go is because whoever they got they information from no longer wanted to talk, so they had nothing."

"I don't like this shit… I don't like it at all."

Frenchie stood up when Paxton started crying and walked into the kitchen to grab a bottle. Soon, his girlfriend,

Elite, came downstairs.

"Hey, P."

"What up, Elite?"

"Give him to me, baby. I'll take him," she told French.

"Nah, he's my son. I got him," he told her.

"Okay, fine. How you feelin', P?" she asked me.

"You know me, just taking shit one day at a time. How's everything at the shop?"

"Those hoes in there drive me crazy, but I love them, and they help me keep the lights on, so I can't complain."

"Oh really? Damn, this whole time I thought it was me who kept your lights on," Frenchie joked.

She playfully punched him in the arm. "Shut up."

"So I'm sayin', P. Like, a nigga is back home, and your ass is out the hospital... What's up with a celebration?"

"That's why I came over here. I'ma call up all our niggas, and we gon' head to the club later tonight, if you're up for it."

"Up for it? Nigga, do you know who you talkin' to?"

"Aight, bet. Well, I'll see you *both* there later tonight."

"Yup. Let me go ahead and see if Mama can watch the kids now. Lord knows I could use a little break," Elite said.

It was a quarter past eleven when we pulled up to the club. As soon as we walked in, it seemed like every Chicago eye was on us. Riot had bitches hanging on him and brought them all over to our private section at the top of the club. Within seconds, we had bottles of liquor, champagne, and weed surrounding us. The BBG brought the party, and everyone was ready to turn up.

"Aight, everybody, grab a mothafuckin' drink," I yelled over the music. "Tonight, we celebrating our nigga French's return home. I want everybody to pour up, light up, and let's show this mothafuckin' city how BBG niggas get down."

The DJ started spinning some music that made all the bitches in the club twerk like their lives depended on it. Every time I looked down over the railing, they would scream like we were NBA stars while their niggas gritted. They either hated us or wanted to be us. Within the first hour of being there, my head was spinning in a sea of Hennessy. I leaned over the railing and pulled out my phone to see that I had a text message from a number I didn't know.

Savannah: Hey, it's me, Savannah.

Pharaoh: What up? You got plans tonight?
Savannah: Nope.
Pharaoh: Come see about a nigga then.
Savannah: And where exactly would I do that?
Pharaoh: The club...802 S. Jefferson Ave.
Savannah: Hmmm...I'm not really a club person, but I'll think about it.
Pharaoh: Think about it?
Savannah: Yeah, that's what I said.
Pharaoh: Don't think too hard, sweetheart. I'll see you in a few.

I locked my phone and an hour passed while I continued to enjoy the party. I turned around when someone tapped me on my shoulder. My eyes landed on a skinny girl wearing a skintight, hot pink spandex mini skirt, a black sequined bra and four-inch heels.

"Can I help you?" I asked.

"Hi... I'm... My name is Lyra."

I nodded. "Pharaoh."

"I know exactly who you are."

I looked her up and down before tossing the rest of my

drink down my throat. She was a cute girl, but she wasn't my type. "Hmm."

She rested her hand on my bicep. "I've been eyeing you all night, and I just had to come up to meet you. I think you're the finest nigga in here, and I would love to spend the rest of the night into the morning with you, if you know what I mean..."

I looked down at the sea of people in the crowd below me, scanning the room. My eyes locked on Savannah, and I licked my lips. She looked picture perfect. She had on a long sleeve black dress that hugged her body in all the right places, and thigh high black boots with her toes peeping out of the front.

"I can't," I said, never even taking my eyes off Savannah.
"Why not?"

"My girl is here," I said and walked right past her.

I quickly made my way downstairs and over to the bar where I saw Savannah sitting. "I see you made the right decision," I whispered in her ear as I stood beside her.

"You said you'd see me later like you were so confident I'd show up, so I almost didn't just to prove you wrong."

"Mmm, and yet, here we are."

"You smell like you've been having a great time," she told me.

"Yeah, shit is like a movie in here tonight."

"That's what you like, huh?"

"Me? Nah."

"No? I kind of find that hard to believe, but I'll play along."

"I'm serious."

"Okay, so what are you celebrating tonight?"

"My family just came home."

"Oh yeah? From where?"

"A place he should've never been, but it's no big deal. That's what niggas keep lawyers on retainer for."

"Ooooh, more rich nigga hood talk," she joked.

"Hey, Pharaoh," a woman said as she passed by me.

"'Sup?" I nodded.

Savannah rolled her eyes and turned her attention to the bar to order a drink. "Let me get a... tequila and pineapple juice."

"I got it," I told her.

"No, I got it. I seem to have a piece of paper with Benjamin Franklin's face on it that's just burning a hole in my purse. Would you like *me* to buy *you* something to drink?"

I chuckled. "You see that up there?" I asked, pointing to the top of the club.

"Yeah."

"That's my section, all of it. We got everything you'd ever want up there, so how about you follow me."

"I think I like it down here with the common folk just fine. Besides, I don't think it matters where I follow you to, your groupies will sniff you out and follow."

"Do I hear some jealousy in your voice?"

"It's not jealousy, just facts."

"Most of the bitches out here are made of plastic... but not you though. I could tell everything on you was real from the moment you walked in here."

"One hundred percent authentic." She smiled.

"I know real when I see it."

Before she had a chance to respond, Frenchie came over to me and threw his arm around my shoulder. "There you are, nigga!"

"What up, fam?"

"Can I holla at you for a minute? It won't take but a second."

"He's all yours," Savannah told him.

"I'll be right back. Don't run off nowhere," I told her.

She turned back to the bar while Frenchie and I stepped away. "What's up?"

"I'm tryna be down again."

"Down with what?"

"Nigga, you already know what."

"You think you ready?"

"Am I?" he asked while pulling two stacks out of his jeans and putting a money phone up to his ear. "Hello? Yeah, man, it's the streets calling. They said they want me back."

I laughed and shook my head. "You know you hot right now. You just came home."

"I know, but I'm ready, my nigga. That's on my soul. I got kids to feed."

I nodded. "Just enjoy the night with your lady and shit. We'll talk business in the morning, aight?"

"Aight, bet. I'll let you get back to whatever it is you were doin' with lil' mama at the bar."

SAVANNAH

Pharaoh came back over to me. "How's your drink?"

"It's fine."

"It's watered down. I can see it. Now, as far as I see, you can come upstairs with me and have real drinks or continue to waste my money down here with that weak shit."

I rolled my eyes. "Fine, let's go."

"Hold onto me so you don't get lost."

I grabbed his arm as he weaved us through the crowd. Every time I locked eyes with a female, she shot me a dirty look as if I'd stolen her dream man. Once we got upstairs, he led us to a secluded area where no one was around and sat down. I sat beside him and poured myself a glass of champagne.

"I'm glad you came out tonight, Savannah."

"Thanks for the invite."

"Exactly how long are you going to be in town?"

"Eh... for a while. No hard dates."

"What brought you to the Chi anyway, if you don't mind me asking?"

"I'm a Russian spy sent to make contact with the CIA to

find out who the mole is in their organization."

"What the fuck?" he said, creasing his forehead in confusion.

"Relax, I'm joking. I just came for work, that's all."

"I might be a little fucked up for those kind of jokes tonight," he told me. "Are you at least enjoying yourself?"

"Yeah, I've never been much of a club girl, but this is cool. At least I get to sit down."

"So you're not one of those girls who I would see twerking in the middle of the floor down there, huh?"

"Nope, I prefer to do my twerking in private."

He nodded. "Noted."

"Look, Pharaoh, I think you're nice and all, but I know what guys like you are all about. You just wanna fuck me to put another notch under your belt. I'm not that type of girl."

"I know. Why you think I gave you my number? That's a privilege not everyone is afforded."

"So what you're saying is I'm special?"

"Yeah. Didn't we go over that earlier?"

I smirked, showing off the dimple in my right cheek. "Anybody ever tell you you're a bit of a smart ass?"

He shrugged. "Maybe once or twice. But for real, these bitches see me, and they see a come up. Whether it's a new bag, a pair of Louboutin heels, whatever. They expect me to afford that shit and wife them up all because they decided to open they legs."

"Sounds like you're out here fuckin' with thot ass bitches."

"But you say you different, right?"

"Hell yeah, I'm different. I don't have time for that shit. I can hold my own. Always have and always will."

"That's what makes you different? What else?"

"What do you mean?"

"You already told me what they said about me in the salon, so now that you're here with me, what do you think I want from you?"

"I already told you what I think you want from me. All niggas are the same, no matter their status. They only want one thing," I told him.

"Sounds like you were just out here fuckin' with some lame ass niggas."

"I think that's the first thing we've agreed upon all night, but lucky for you, I'm not fuckin' with them anymore. I'm not fuckin' with anybody actually."

"And why is that?"

I tossed the rest of the champagne in my glass down my throat and set the flute on the table. "To make a long story short, I gave the wrong people the right pieces of me until I didn't have anything left. So, I've been celibate for... a while now. Just really trying not to get my heart broken again."

"Who would be dumb enough to break your heart?" he asked.

"You'd be surprised."

"Well, you don't have to worry about that with me because I'm definitely not the type of nigga who is trying to steal your heart."

"Exactly what type of nigga are you then?"

"I think you already know the answer to that."

He looked me in my eyes, and I froze. If he was trouble, it never looked so damn good.

"I got some shit on my face or something?" he asked.

"What? No."

"What you lookin' at then?"

"I don't know... There's something about you... I just haven't decided if it's good or bad yet."

He flashed a smile at me. "It's a perfect mixture of both."

"Hmm, noted. What time is it?"

"Almost two. The club about to close soon."

"I think I'm about to head back home. I'm getting tired."

"The night is just beginning for me. I don't really sleep too much at night anyway." He shrugged.

"Why not? Does your mind keep a lot of tabs open or somethin'?"

"Yeah, you could say that."

I stood to my feet, and he stared up at me, eyeing me from head to toe. My eyes were fixated on his juicy lips as he licked them.

"You gon' walk me out or keep droolin'?" I asked.

He smirked as he stood up. "Of course."

Once again, Pharaoh led us through the club and outside to inhale the city's night air. He leaned against the side of the brick building while I set up my Uber to get home.

"My ride is about five minutes away," I told him. "You can go back inside. I'll be good."

"A lot can happen around here in five minutes. Besides, I ain't in no rush to get back in there anyway. As far as I'm concerned, the party is over."

"Why is that?"

"Because you're leaving," he admitted.

"I don't know much about me being the party. I'm just a city girl trapped in a country girl's body, who doesn't know how to climb trees or catch lightning bugs." I belted out a nervous laugh then quickly sucked in air while covering my mouth.

"All that, huh?"

"My bad."

"You good."

The bright headlights from a red Nissan Versa shone past me, and I turned back to look at Pharaoh for the last time that night. "My ride is here."

He displayed a wide grin and nodded. "Goodnight, Savannah."

"Goodnight."

Chapter Six

FRANCES "FRENCHIE" BLACKWELL

As soon as I was a free man again, the first thing I wanted to do was get back to the money. The only way I knew how to do that was to dive head first back into the drug business with Pharaoh. I'd been a product of the streets since I was thirteen years old. Hustlin', schemin', slangin', and robbin' were in my blood.

Soon, I started reppin' the Big Bank Gang. I took a blood oath to prove my loyalty, and I would bleed BBG until the day I took my last fuckin' breath. The night I got hemmed up by the police, I didn't even trip. I knew I had the respect and the protection of my BBG niggas on the inside while Pharaoh was on the outside pullin' all the legal strings to get me back home. The moment the cops said LaDavius Millwood's name, I knew they were going to try to throw my ass underneath the jail. My old hitta needed his ass handled, and I put two bullets in his brain without even blinkin'.

"What you over there thinkin' about, baby?" Elite whispered in my ear.

"Shit, nothin'."

"You havin' a good time?" she asked.

I turned the Ace of Spades bottle up to my lips. She already knew the answer. I was off the shits, having a good time. She smiled and ran her hand over my beard.

"I'm so happy you're back, baby. The kids and I really missed you."

"You know they can't keep a good nigga down for too long, baby," I said, kissing her cheeks.

"I love you, French."

"You know I love you, too, Elite. Enough talking; let's celebrate. Pour up with your nigga."

Elite smiled and grabbed a shot glass full of tequila. "I guess it's gonna be a pump and dump kind of night." She giggled and then threw the shot back.

"That's what I like to see. Come here, girl."

I spun Elite around, and she pushed her juicy ass against my dick and started grinding to the bass. I rested my left hand on her waist and turned the bottle up to my lips again. Just before the song ended, a nigga bumped into me.

"Yo, watch the fuck out, nigga," I said, shrugging his light-skinned ass off me.

"Chill, nigga. We in the fuckin' club. What you expect?"

"You heard what the fuck I said. You see me and my fuckin' girl dancin' and shit."

"Man, fuck you and your bitch, nigga," he mumbled.

My eyes narrowed as I looked him up and down and stepped closer to him. "What the fuck you say?"

"Man, nigga, you heard me," he grunted.

I sized his ass up and tightened my grip around the bottle neck in my hand. All I could see was me spillin' that nigga's blood all over the dance floor. As soon as I lifted my arm, Pharaoh caught it.

"Hold up. Is there a problem here, nigga?" he asked, stepping in front of me.

"Nigga disrespecting my girl like he don't know I'll rag tag his fuckin' ass. Don't you know this BBG territory in here?" I shouted.

I watched him look around at myself, Pharaoh, and the gang of hittas that had formed a wall behind us. I knew his pussy ass thought he was dealin' with a regular ass nigga when he stepped to me, and I was gon' show his ass just how wrong he was.

"Yo, French. Just chill, my nigga. We celebratin' tonight," Pharaoh told me.

"Fuck that! This nigga looking at me funny, like he got something he wanna fuckin' say."

"I said what I had to say, n—"

Before he even finished his sentence, I stole off on his ass and knocked him two feet back. I charged at him, and P pulled me off his ass for disrespecting me, Elite, and my niggas.

"Nah, niggas wanna go toe to toe with me in the streets like I'm a pussy or somethin'! I bleed this gang shit! BBG 'til I mothafuckin' die, and that's on my fuckin' kids, nigga!" I yelled as Pharaoh pulled me away.

In the blink of an eye, all my BBG niggas started beatin' the shit out of that light-skinned nigga and his boys. Pharaoh shoved me out the side door of the club.

"What the fuck is wrong with you, nigga? You just got out of fuckin' jail less than twenty-four hours ago, and you tryna set yourself up to go right the fuck back!" Pharaoh yelled.

"I don't give a fuck about that jail shit, nigga. You already know that!"

"Baby, please, just stop!" Elite said, grabbing my hand.

I shooed her away. "Get the fuck off me, Elite, and go home!"

"Let's go home together, baby. It's late," she pleaded.

"You know me well enough to know I ain't goin' no mothafuckin' where until I split that nigga's head wide open."

"You already hit the nigga. Just let it go."

"That was just a taste. I can't wait until him and his niggas come out that bitch. I'm 'bout to light them niggas up like it's the mothafuckin' Fourth," I said, lifting up my shirt, brandishing my pistol.

PHARAOH

I shot my eyes over at Frenchie and shook my head. I knew that once his mind was made up, there was no such thing as trying to make him have a change of heart.

"So is you ridin' with me or what?" he asked me.

"P, no! You need to stop him! Please!" Elite begged.

I looked at her and then looked back at French. He was my blood, and I wasn't gon' have him go out lookin' for trouble alone. My life consisted of gunshots, drugs, and gang wars. Every time I turned around, niggas had they hand out for money or they hands crossed in a casket. I wanted better. I always had. But I wasn't gon' get it that night.

"Go home, Elite," I said, pulling my gun out from the back of my jeans.

"I swear to God you're so mothafuckin' selfish, French! What about me? What about your kids, huh? You just tryna find a reason to get killed!" she fumed.

"I won't let anything happen to him," I promised her.

"I would expect this irrational shit from him, P, but not you. You need to stop him."

"Goodnight, Elite."

She rolled her teary eyes and shot a look at French, who wouldn't even make eye contact with her. She quickly spun around on her heels, and we both watched her walk down the sidewalk to the car. Neither of us said a word until she started the engine and sped off.

"She's right, you know. You bein' selfish as fuck right now."

"I know. Don't change shit though."

Not only was Frenchie my family, he was my best friend. Most of the time, I knew what he was thinking before he did. We were cut from the same cloth and raised in a city where every vice you could think of was plotting against you. Livin' life on the edge was all the nigga knew how to do.

The two of us went over to my car and sat inside to wait for the club to let out.

"Yo, who was that girl you were talkin' to earlier?" he asked.

"What girl?"

"Nigga, you know damn well what girl."

"Nah, she cool. Met her at the hospital when I was in there. She was in a plane crash."

"And she survived? Nah, nigga, you gotta leave that bitch alone. She probably a witch or somethin'," he joked.

"Nigga, what?" I chuckled.

"How many people you know survive whole airplane crashes without a scratch?"

"She didn't make it out without a scratch, nigga. You don't even know what you're talkin' about. You're drunk."

"Shit, she ain't look scratched up to me."

"You just ain't look hard enough."

"Should I be?"

"No, nigga. Don't look her way."

"That's what I thought. I know you feelin' her. Yo, when that nigga Rico supposed to be comin' back?"

"His grandma died, so he went down to Atlanta to be with his family for a little bit. I'ma call him in the morning and see what's up."

He nodded and focused his attention on the flood of people that were flowing out of the side door of the club. Our eyes sifted through all the faces, some familiar, some not, until they landed on Frenchie's target.

"There that nigga go right there," he said to me, while holding his gun in his lap.

"Do you see that nigga? He can barely walk? The hittas fucked him up enough already," I said with reason in my voice.

"Fuck walkin'. I wanna make sure that nigga never speaks again," he grumbled.

The two of us sat in silence and watched him and two of his niggas make their way down the street to the navy-blue Chevy Impala they were driving. Once they were inside, I started the engine and pulled off. He reached into my glove compartment and pulled out two ski masks.

"You ready?" he asked while pulling the mask over his face.

We exchanged knowing looks at each other, and I nodded while putting my mask on. "Let's do this shit."

French and I followed them all the way to a stoplight, where I pulled up on their left side. The driver revved his engine and glanced over at us. That's when Frenchie rolled down his window.

"What up, niggas?" Frenchie asked and started spraying their car with bullets.

As soon as the light turned green, I sped off down the

road while their car remained still. They were all dead. I glanced down at the smoke seeping out the barrel of French's gun, and alongside the adrenaline pumping through my body, I felt relieved that it was over, and that we were the ones standing in the end. I whipped my car through the city and didn't stop until I made it to French's house. I made a promise to Elite to keep him safe, and that's what I did.

When the car came to a complete stop, I turned my attention to him. "Stay the fuck out of trouble, nigga."

"You know trouble is my middle name." He smirked and shut the door behind him.

THE SECOND I stepped foot into my spot, I pulled out my phone and texted Savannah. I knew it was late, but I didn't care.

Pharaoh: Did you make it home okay?

Savannah: Yeah, you?

Pharaoh: Yeah. Just got in.

Savannah: Good. I'll talk to you tomorrow. Goodnight.

Those were the last words I read before passing out across my bed. I woke up the next morning with another text from her.

Savannah: How was last night?

Pharaoh: Crazy. I'm glad you left when you did.

Savannah: Why? What happened?

Pharaoh: Some shit popped off.

Savannah: Like what?

Pharaoh: Meet up with me today and I'll tell you in person.

Savannah: Oh yeah?

Pharaoh: Yeah.

Savannah: Only if you take me to the best place to eat out here.

I'm starving.

Pharaoh: Bet. I got some business to handle first. Start getting ready and send me your address. I'll text you when I'm on my way.

I got up and headed straight to the shower to get dressed. Once I got myself together, I headed back over to Elite and Frenchie's house to check in on him and talk business. As soon as I knocked, I heard Elite's voice on the other side yelling for me to come in. I walked in and saw Elite feeding the baby while Imani was eating some chicken nuggets and watching cartoons.

"What up, Elite? Where French at?"

"Downstairs."

"Aight, bet. You good after last night?"

She shrugged and rolled her eyes. "It's over now. What else can I do about it?"

I saw the sadness and annoyance in her eyes and decided it was best to let her go back to what she was doing without my distraction. I headed downstairs to the basement and saw French sitting on the couch watching TV.

"What up, P?" he asked when he turned to look my way.

I sat on the opposite couch. "'Sup?"

"You good?"

"Nigga, I should be asking you that. What the hell was that shit about last night, huh? All because a nigga bumped you in the club?"

"It started as that, but then the nigga started disrespecting me, so I had to show his ass what was really good, you feel me?"

I shook my head. "Fuck all that, nigga. You got two strikes over your head. You don't want to just let these niggas hand you your third one. You gotta be smarter than that, especially if you wanna get back down."

Frenchie let his head drop to his lap before raising his neck to look at me. "You right, fam. I know I gotta do better and calm my rowdy ass down. It's just hard. You know I'm always on go no matter what."

"There's a time and a place, French. That's all I'm sayin'."

"Now you sound like Big Mama, nigga." He chuckled.

"Hey, she raised us, didn't she?"

"Aight, nigga, but I hear you though, for real. I do. I'ma try and get my shit together."

"Bet. I'ma hit you when I want you to meet me at the spot, and we'll get your ass back to work," I said, dapping him up.

Frenchie nodded. "Bet. Love you, fam."

"Love you, too."

I said my goodbyes to Elite and the kids and headed back out to my car. I checked my phone to see if I'd gotten a text back from Savannah with her address and I never did, so I called her.

"Hello?" she answered.

"What's up? You ready?"

"Yeah, I'm ready."

"Then why you didn't send me your address?"

"Because I'm not sure if I want you to know where I live just yet."

"Damn, what you think, a nigga is gon' stalk you or somethin'?"

"I mean… I haven't been in Chicago that long, and you are the one person I seem to run into all the time."

"The city is small. What you want me to do about that?" I asked.

She chuckled. "Mm hmm. Okay. I'll text you my address in a second."

I ended the call, and once I got her address, I headed over to pick her up. Savannah came out of the building looking like a breath of fresh air. As soon as she got inside my blacked-out Tesla, her fragrance filled the entire car.

"Damn, you smell good as hell," I told her.

She smiled. "Thank you. So where are you taking me to eat? I'm starving."

"That depends on what you're in the mood for. Do you want soul food, Italian, American, what?"

"You know what, take me to get some Chicago pizza." I rolled my eyes, and she looked at me. "What?"

"All that tourist talk... it's cute," I joked.

"Whatever."

"If it's pizza you want, then it's pizza you'll get."

She rested her head back against the seat and looked out of the window. "Thank you."

The waiter seated us in a booth that was in a secluded section of the restaurant. Whenever I went out to eat, I didn't like to be around a lot of people if I could help it. Once we put in our order, I watched her put her straw in her drink and take a sip.

"Damn, this margarita is really good."

"I'm glad you like it."

"Why didn't you get one? Too many drinks from last night?"

"Something like that."

"Finish telling me about last night. You told me you'd tell me when we were face to face."

I ran my hand down my face and shook my head. "My cousin, you know the one that I told you just came home, he got into it with some dude who bumped into him, and it was a whole big thing, that's all."

"Like a fight?"

"Yeah."

"Were you involved it?"

"Nah. I really don't like to get my hands dirty if I don't have to. I used to be a hot-headed nigga, but not so much now as I get older."

"But it seems like your cousin does."

I shrugged. "We come from the same place, but we think differently, that's all."

"You said you used to be a hot head. What changed you?"
"The streets... life. All of it."
"You're weird, you know that?"
"Weird? How?"
"I don't know. It's like you're an open book and a mystery all at the same time."
"I don't think anybody has ever said that to me before." I chuckled.
"No, I mean, I only say it's weird because I just want to know more, but at the same time, I don't want to pry. Your business isn't any of my business."
"What do you want to know?"
"I don't know... Start from the beginning," she told me.
"If I tell you about me, then you gotta go next and tell me about you. Deal?"
She nodded. "Deal."
I drew in a deep breath and then exhaled. "My cousin and I were both raised by our grandmother. Her name was Dolly, but we called her Big Mama. Although we were cousins, we grew up more like brothers. He's two years older than me, so you already

know my young ass was gettin' all the hand-me-downs and everything, whether it was clothes, shoes, toys, whatever."

"What happened to both of your parents?" she asked.

"Our mothers were sisters. His mother was killed by his father, and he was taken to jail. My mother left me on Big Mama's front porch when I was four years old, and I ain't seen her ass since. As far as my pops, never knew the nigga."

"I'm so sorry. That must've been so hard for you."

"Nah, not really. You can't miss what you never had. Big Mama had enough love for the both of us. We were her only two grandchildren, and she raised us as good as she could up until she got sick. That's when shit started to go downhill. The worse her cancer got, the higher her medical bills and pill prescriptions got. All she was getting was a few hundred dollars from the government every month, and that wasn't doin' shit. So, I decided to get my hands dirty."

"What do you mean? Like selling drugs or somethin'?"

"Yeah, I sold dope. A young nigga had cornrows and everything back then." He chuckled. "But it got the bills paid."

"How old were you when you were doing all this?"

"High school…"

"And where was your cousin?"

"He was already knee-deep into his own shit. I didn't have time to wait around on him. If I did that, both me and Big Mama would've been out on the street somewhere."

"So what about school? Did you drop out to take care of your grandma?"

"Nah. She wouldn't let me. Somehow, I balanced school, basketball, dealin', and takin' care of her."

"Wow, so you were still able to graduate?"

"Yeah. I had a college acceptance letter and a full scholarship to get me the fuck outta here to play ball for a D-1 school and everything, but by the time I graduated, I was knee-deep in the streets, and I couldn't get out. To be honest, the only thing I was better at than basketball was sellin' drugs."

"Whatever happened to your grandma?"

"She passed about four months after my graduation. To this day, I still don't know if it was the cancer or the heartbreak of me not goin' off to college that killed her."

I looked in her face and her eyes were glassy as if she was about to cry. "You aight?"

"Yeah, I… I don't know. I guess I never heard someone be so honest before, or at least I didn't expect it. It was refreshing. Thank you."

"For what?"

"For sharing that with me. I thought you were gonna be like, oh, my name is Pharaoh, and I like fast cars and shit," she said, trying to make her voice deeper.

I laughed at her. "You funny, but now it's your turn."

"I don't know if there's anything I could say about myself that would live up to even half of what you just told me."

"Don't worry about all that. Just tell me anything."

"Well, my name is Savannah, and I'm a sucker for s'mores and Girl Scout cookies." She giggled.

"I don't think I've ever eaten a s'more in my life. Ain't that like the marshmallow shit?"

"Yes, and chocolate and graham crackers. It's like a sweet ass sandwich," she joked. "I used to be the top s'more maker on the east coast, scouts honor."

"Bullshit."

"Not bullshit. I was a proud member of troop 448!" She chuckled.

"You wild. Maybe you can make one for me one day then. Let me see what skills you got."

She flashed a smile at me. "Deal."

The waiter brought over our pizza, and we started eating. "Can I ask you something?" she asked.

"What's up?"

"Do you do this often?"

"What?"

"Take girls out on dates?"

"I wasn't aware this was a date, Savannah."

Her face went blank for a few seconds, and I knew I had her. Even if she tried to forget me, I knew she never would. She quickly recovered with an eye roll and a smile. "I'm glad you let me know."

"I'm kidding... And no, I don't do this often. I don't do this ever," I admitted.

"Good to know."

My phone began to vibrate face down on the table, and I ignored it. It vibrated again, and I glanced down at it. "Back to back calls usually means you should answer your phone," she told me.

I flipped the phone over and answered Riot's call. "What up?"

"Where are you?"

"Eating."

"Well put the fork down nigga and get over to the crib. I just got some fucked up news."

"What happened?" I asked, tightening my grip on the phone.

"Man, Big City got killed in Terror Town about an hour ago."

"What?"

"Yeah, man. I can't believe my big nigga got life in a pine box."

"You know how it happened?"

"I'd rather not say over the line."

I nodded. "Don't worry, we gon' take care of all of it."

"I'll see you when you get here."

"Aight, bet. Keep your head up," I told him and ended the call.

"Bad news?" Savannah asked, flashing her long eyelashes up at me.

"Huh?"

"On the phone... You look like you got some bad news."

"Yeah, um... I gotta go."

"What happened?"

"My friend was killed an hour ago."

"What? Oh my God, I'm so sorry."

"Yeah, I gotta get over there."

"No, I completely understand."

"I can drop you off at home first."

She nodded, and I paid the check. The two of us hurried out of the restaurant, and I took her back to her spot. Before she got out of the car, she turned to me. "Thank you for the pizza, and again, I'm really sorry to hear about your friend."

"Yeah, thanks. Me too."

"Let me know if you need anything."

"Thank you, and I'm sorry I had to cut today short. I'll make it up to you, I promise."

She smiled. "I know you will."

As soon as she got out of the car, I sped off and headed over to Riot's place to put together how we were gon' get back at the niggas who took a BBG hitta's life.

Chapter Seven

PHARAOH

I pulled my car into Riot's driveway and darted into the house. "What the fuck happened?" I yelled.

Frenchie was sitting on the couch. He didn't even flinch when I burst through the door. "Riot said the nigga hit a stain over in Terror Town and got done up on the spot."

"Who the fuck did he rob?"

He shrugged. "He stole some nigga's car. He jumped in that shit, sped off, and niggas chased him. When he pulled up at the light, they pulled up right beside him and lit his ass up."

My muscles tightened as I balled my hands into fists. "Who the fuck did it?"

"Riot on the phone with some of the hittas now. He'll be back in a minute. You want a beer or somethin'?"

I plopped down on the couch and shook my head. "I need something stronger than a fuckin' beer, nigga."

"Say no more," he said, passing me a bottle of Hennessy.

I grabbed the bottle and took it straight to the face. I glanced over at Frenchie as he lit his freshly rolled blunt. "Yo, you good?" I asked him.

Frenchie shrugged. "Nah. That shit got me fucked up, for real."

"What the fuck was that nigga even doin' tryna steal a fuckin' car? Niggas act like everybody in BBG wasn't out here eatin' good."

"Sometimes eatin' ain't enough. Sometimes a nigga wanna feel that real shit to get the adrenaline pumpin' again," he told me.

I let out an aggravated sigh and watched Riot walk through his back door. "What up, P?"

"Shit. What's the word?"

Riot sat down on the couch beside me and shook his head. "Word is Big City got lit up by some MCF niggas."

My forehead creased. "Man, fuck them Money Comes First niggas."

"Just say the word and we out."

"Oh, we definitely gon' go see about them niggas."

"Yo, you heard from that nigga Rico?" Frenchie asked.

"Yeah, I forgot to tell you I talked to him on the way over here. His plane lands in an hour, and the nigga said he's down for whatever."

"Bet. We gon' have to show these niggas what the fuck is really up." Riot nodded.

THE THREE OF us sat around talkin' until my phone vibrated.

"Yo, Rico's flight just landed. Let's go pick this nigga up from the airport and then go handle these niggas," I told them.

Once we were all in the car, Frenchie looked in the back seat and looked at Riot. "Nigga, who the fuck you textin' at a time like this?"

"Yo, shut up, nigga. I'm just settin' up some shit for after we handle these niggas."

"What kinda shit?"

"Nigga, you already know what's up. After this shit, a nigga gon' need a hot shower, a blunt, and some bomb ass head to relax."

I shook my head. As wild as Riot was, he had a point. I'd been thinking of my own ways to unwind after we handled what we had to do for Big City's death.

"You a stupid ass nigga," Frenchie said as he loaded his gun from the passenger seat.

"What can I say? I met this bitch at the club a few weeks back, and she bad as fuck. I mean from her head to her pretty ass feet. I'm tryna dig all in that shit later, and if that don't work, I just started fuckin' on this bitch that work at the post office."

Frenchie's entire face screwed up. "Nigga, you fuckin' a mail lady?"

"Hell yeah! Listen to the logic, nigga! The bitch work for the post office. That means I can get her to ship and deliver my shit on her carrier route."

"What you pay her?"

"Pay her? Nigga, what you mean? My dick is my currency," he said, grabbing hold of his balls.

"This nigga wild," Frenchie said while relighting his blunt.

"Nah, I ain't e'en gotta pay her because the bitch already on the clock!"

"Nigga, anybody ever tell you all you do is talk about sex?" I asked him.

"Yeah, and? Shit, that's all I do is fuck bitches, smoke good weed, and get money. The hood nigga's holy trinity," he joked.

We pulled up to the airport, and I pulled out my phone to call Rico. As soon as he got inside, French and I both looked back at him. "You down to ride, nigga?" I asked him.

"Yeah."

"Good, now take this pistol."

"Riot, you got an address?" Rico asked.

"Yeah, I do."

"What is it?" I asked.

Riot passed his phone to me, and I put the address in. Twenty minutes later, I made a right turn down the street and shut the lights off. I glanced over at French and watched him sprinkle some white powder in a dollar bill, hold it up to his nose, and sniff hard. "Nigga, what the fuck is you doing?"

He cut his eyes at me. "Just getting my head in the game, that's all. Damn, nigga, chill."

"Y'all niggas ready?" I asked.

"Hell yeah. This one is for Big City," Riot said, cocking his gun.

I looked back at Rico and then over at French. They both nodded at me. "Let's go make these MCF niggas' blood flow like Lake Michigan," I told them.

SAVANNAH

My phone vibrated against my nightstand at a quarter 'til midnight. I rolled over and saw that Pharaoh was calling. I quickly cleared my throat and answered. "H-hello?"

"You sleep?"

"Almost," I admitted.

"Look, I know it's late, but I was wondering if I could see you so we could finish what we started earlier."

I pulled the phone away from my ear. I knew the hours of eleven o'clock at night to three o'clock in the morning were booty call hours, and I wasn't about to go out like that. "It's late, Pharaoh."

"I know..."

"But... I guess you could come over for a little bit. Just know you ain't gettin' nothin' but a handshake at the end of the night."

"I'm cool with that."

"Okay. How far away are you?"

"I'll be there in... thirty minutes. Just droppin' my boys off. I'll call you when I'm out front."

I nodded. "Okay."

I quickly shot up out of the bed and ran through the house lighting candles, spraying Febreze, and making sure the apartment looked as good as it did the first day I stepped inside it. After that, I took my scarf off my head, shook out my hair, and darted into the kitchen to pull out the fresh package of marshmallows, Hershey's chocolate bars, and an unopened box of graham crackers I'd bought earlier that day. I threw on a pair of Victoria's Secret sweatpants and a racerback tank top and turned on the TV in the living room, when my phone vibrated again.

"Hello?"

"What's up? I'm outside."

"I'll buzz you in now. I'm on the twelfth floor, apartment 1222."

"Bet. I'm comin' up," he said and ended the call.

My heartbeat quickened when I heard him knocking on the other side of the door. I ran my hands down the front of my sweatpants and then unlocked the door. I smiled as soon as my eyes locked on his.

"Hey."

"What's up?"

"Come in," I told him as I stood to the side.

Pharaoh walked in and looked around. "Your spot is nice."

"Thank you."

"What is it that you do again?"

"I could be asking you the same thing."

"Touché."

"Come in the kitchen. I've got a surprise for you."

"I think I've had enough surprises for the day," he said, rubbing the back of his neck.

"It's a good surprise, I promise."

Pharaoh followed me into the kitchen, and I flipped on the lights and pointed to the countertop. "Ta-Da!" I cheered.

"What the hell is this?"

I sucked my teeth. "It's all the ingredients you need to make s'mores!"

He balled his hand into a fist and put it out to his mouth. "Oh shit. Wow, what the fuck, Savannah?"

I giggled. "After I told you about my obsession with s'mores, I started craving them! So after you dropped me off, I went back out to the store and grabbed everything. I was gon' wait until tomorrow to make a couple, but when you called and asked to come over, I thought why not?"

He smiled. "So you gon' show me how to make one since you supposed to be the best s'more maker alive, right?"

"Yeah, come on."

I turned on the stove and pulled two barbeque skewers

out of the drawer to hand him one. I stuck the marshmallows on the ends and held them over the heat until they were a little burnt, then placed it on top of a piece of chocolate and the graham cracker. "Now bite into it," I told him.

He examined the gooey goodness and then took a small bite. "Hmm."

"Well?"

"This shit good as fuck." He laughed.

"See, I told you! Now give me my props," I bragged.

"Aight, you got it. This is probably the best shit I've ever tasted."

I made us both a couple more, and we propped ourselves up on the countertop and ate them. "Did you check on your friends?" I asked him.

"Yeah, I did."

"How is everybody taking the news? How are you taking the news?"

"One second of every minute of every hour of every day at a time."

I nodded. "I can only imagine how hard it is. Were the two of you super close?"

"Close enough. It's crazy. It's like everybody looks to me for guidance all the fuckin' time, and sometimes a nigga just be wantin' to fade into the background and take my hands off the wheel for just a second, but that never happens."

"They must look to you for a reason, Pharaoh. You're probably like a leader to them."

"The crown is heavy, Savannah. When you winning, you need to know the difference between who is riding with you and who is riding for you. Sometimes, it's just not that easy to tell."

"What do you think will happen if you ever take your hands off the wheel?"

"I don't know, and I'll probably never find out. I don't do well when I'm not in control."

"Where do you think you got such strong leadership qualities from?"

He let his shoulders rise and fall. "I don't know. It's not like I grew up looking up to anyone; I just saw a lot of niggas who I knew I didn't want to be nothin' like. Role models of what not the fuck to be."

I nodded, and he continued. "I grew up under niggas who jacked niggas for a livin' and sometimes even for fun. My cousin got caught tryna rob a corner store for everything in the cash drawer. He lucky his ass was a minor at the time because if he'd been an adult, they would've given his ass three years for that shit, and it wasn't even five hundred fuckin' dollars."

"What do you want to do that's different?"

"Shit that can help the people who help me. Nobody ever talks about niggas giving to charities or shelters, rebuilding the fuckin' city we keep tearin' down, feeding the homeless or the kids. I wanna do shit like that."

"Then what's stoppin' you?" I asked.

"My niggas keep dyin', and I'm left to tie up all the loose ends. The streets ain't lettin' a nigga like me go."

I shook my head and turned my attention to the TV where a commercial was playing. I honestly didn't know what to say to him. Not only was Pharaoh's honesty refreshing, it was a turn on. I'd never been with a man who could talk his talk without me seeing right through it.

"But enough about all that sad shit."

"Yeah, I'm sorry. I didn't mean to bring the mood down with all my questions," I told him.

I looked down at the plate and shook my head. What had started as a midnight snack soon turned into comfort food while I listened to his sad story about his friend and his adolescent years.

"Nah, you good. I don't ever get to talk about that type of shit."

"Really? Why not?"

"Nobody to talk to. I'm a private nigga, Savannah, but... I don't know. You bringin' out somethin' different in me."

"Like what?"

He shrugged. "You make me wanna let somebody in."

"Somebody or me?"

"I don't know yet." He smirked.

"Mmm, noted."

"At least a few good things happened to me today."

"Oh yeah? Like what?"

"Well, I got to see you, and my boy Rico came back today, and I got to see you again."

"Rico?"

"Yeah, he's another one of my boys. He just came back from burying his grandmother in Atlanta. He's been gon' for a while, too, but I understand how families work, so I let him do him."

"Hmm."

"What?"

I hopped off the countertop and rested my back against the refrigerator. "I don't know. You said the name Rico, and something in my mind clicked, but I don't know why the name sounds so familiar."

"You think it's some of your memory comin' back?" he asked.

I looked at him with my eyebrows knitted. "I don't know... It's like it's right on the tip of my tongue, and I just can't figure it out."

"Don't stress about it. It'll all come back to you when it's supposed to."

I nodded. "You're right."

"Damn, it's late as hell," he said, looking at his phone for the first time that night.

"What time is it?" I asked.

"Almost four o'clock in the morning."

"Wow. I feel like you just got here."

"Yeah, me too. I won't keep you up all night though... unless..."

"Unless... what?"

"Nah, I'm fuckin' with you. I'll hit you up tomorrow."

"You sure you good to drive home?"

"I'm not high or drunk off s'mores, Savannah. I'm good. I'm a night owl anyway, remember?"

"That's right, the brain tabs," I said, smacking my forehead.

Pharaoh gently grabbed my hand and pulled it away from my head. "Don't do that."

"Why not?"

"I don't want you hurtin' anything on that beautiful face of yours," he said as he slid the back of his hand down my cheek.

I flashed my eyes up toward his. The more interactions we had with each other, the more I wanted him. Craved him even. I started gently sliding my bottom lip in between my teeth, and he ran his thumb down the front of my lips. "Kiss me, Pharaoh," I told him.

Without hesitation, he pulled my lips onto his, and fireworks exploded inside my body. The way his lips attached to mine made me feel like he never wanted to let me go. I ran my hands up his biceps to peak at his shoulder blades as he ran his hands down my waist and squeezed me. By the time he pulled away, my entire body felt like it'd been set on fire.

"Goodnight, Savannah," he told me while licking his lips.

"Goodnight..."

ELITE KNIGHT

I'd been with Frenchie for six years. We were only together for six months before I got pregnant with our daughter,

Imani, and our son Paxton was eight weeks old. I loved Frenchie, but I was done with the babies; I wanted a ring. I was sitting in the living room, feeding the baby, when I darted my attention to the front door. After loudly fumbling with the lock on the front door, Frenchie finally entered the house.

I watched him stumble inside and drop his keys on the floor. He bent over to pick them up and looked at me on his way up.

"Shit, girl. You scared me. What are you doing up?"

"It's four o'clock in the morning, and we have a newborn. You do the math."

"I don't need the attitude, Elite."

"Where have you been?"

"What you mean where I been? I'm a grown ass man," he said, slouching on the sofa.

I shot him a venomous look. He smelled like weed and alcohol, which made me want to throw up. I got up and moved over to the other couch. "What's your problem?"

"You fuckin' stink, Frenchie."

"Oh." He shrugged nonchalantly.

I sucked my teeth. "Just go upstairs and go to bed," I told him.

"Can't sleep. I'm too fuckin' high to sleep."

I rolled my eyes and stood up to take the baby upstairs. "Fine. Stay your stupid ass down here on the couch then."

"Yo, Elite, what the fuck is your problem?" he yelled. "Damn! You blowin' me, and I ain't even been in this mothafucka for five minutes!"

I stormed up the stairs to put Paxton in his crib, gently closed the door, and went back downstairs. "You wanna know what my problem is, nigga? Ever since your ass got out of jail, all you do is go out with your boys every night, knowing damn well you have two kids at home! You always do this shit!"

"Do what? What the fuck did I do?"

"When we're makin' the baby, you wanna be a fuckin' family man, and then as soon as the baby gets here, you act like you're fuckin' fourteen years old again! You did it with Imani, and you're doing it with Paxton! You probably did it with your other son, too!"

Frenchie's nostrils flared as he shot a cold glance in my direction. "Fuck you, Elite."

"Fuck me? Nigga, fuck you! Like I said, stay your stupid mothafuckin' ass down here!" I said, storming up the stairs and slamming the door to our bedroom.

I was fuming. Being Frenchie Blackwell's girl used to be everything to me. There was something about the thug in him that made my pussy so wet. That, and his powerful reputation in the BBG. I knew he was a killer when I met him, and I was down for the ride right up until I got pregnant. Two kids later, and it just wasn't as easy to walk away.

I laid on top of the covers and stared at the ceiling. He must've thought I was a fool. Ain't no way a nigga had all of this at home waitin' on his ass every day and he just willingly left the money on the table. I shot up and threw my legs over the side of the bed. I crept out of the room and peered down over the banister into the living room from the top of the stairs. He'd finally fallen asleep on the couch. I tiptoed down the stairs, grabbed his phone, and went back upstairs to our room. I spent the next hour going through every text message thread and call logs.

I woke up a few hours later to Paxton crying on the baby monitor. My eyes opened, and I realized I'd passed out on top of the covers with Frenchie's phone on my chest. My feet shuffled out of the bedroom and into Paxton's room.

"Hi, baby boy," I said, picking him up. "Good morning."

"I got 'em," Frenchie said from behind me.

I turned to see him leaning against the door frame and rolled my eyes. "Nah, you good."

"Give me my son, Elite, and stop fuckin' with me."

"Fine, and once you're done with him, you can come explain to me why you're still fuckin' your other baby mama."

His forehead creased. "What the fuck are you talkin' about?"

"You know exactly what I'm talking about. When are you gon' stop playin' me for a fuckin' fool?"

Frenchie rubbed his eye and then brushed past me. "Man, watch out."

I walked back into the room and into the bathroom. With

my back pressed against the door, I grabbed a piece of toilet paper and dabbed my eyes. I hovered over the sink, refusing to look myself in the mirror. "Just walk away, E," I whispered to myself.

"Mommy?"

I heard Imani's tiny voice on the other side of the door, and my heart broke completely. "Y-yeah, baby girl?"

"Are you okay?"

"I'm okay, baby. Mommy is okay."

"Can I come in?"

I exhaled and closed my eyes. "Sure."

I stepped away from the door and let Imani in. I walked over and sat on top of the toilet, and she wrapped her arms around my neck. "Don't cry, Mommy."

I nodded my head. "I'm not crying," I said as my voice shook.

"I love you."

"I love you, too, Mani Boo!"

I hugged her and smiled. I was supposed to be the one taking care of her, but little did she know, she was my rock. My five-year-old rock.

"Mani, let me talk to your mommy real quick," Frenchie told her from the doorway.

She looked back at me for approval, and I nodded. "Go tell your baby brother good morning."

She scurried out of the bathroom, and Frenchie closed the door behind her. I turned my back to him and looked toward the shower. "What do you want?"

He sucked his teeth. "Why the fuck are you cryin'?"

I shot my fiery eyes at him. "Just tell me the truth, Frenchie. Are you still fuckin' her?"

"I'm not fuckin' nobody but you, Elite, damn."

"Then why the fuck does the bitch text you every fuckin' day?"

"We got a fuckin' son together! I know your nosy ass went through my phone! You read the messages, so you already know what the fuck is up!"

"Yeah, and I know you just don't be talkin' about Junior either, nigga!"

"Look, she said my son need a fuckin' winter jacket. I can't have my seed runnin' around with a fuckin' runny nose and shit."

"She's always askin' for money! You are the father of her son, not her sponsor. I see her all the time on Facebook, fronting and shit. She's not gettin' another dime until we can prove it's going to the betterment of your son and not in her goddamn pocket! We have a family of our own to take care of. It's bad enough we were pregnant at damn near the same time. Now I gotta share you twenty-four-seven with the bitch, too?"

"I've been locked up. What the fuck you want me to do?"

"Either you gon' tell her, or I'm gonna snatch the bitch up myself."

He sighed. "Fine, I'll talk to her. Just stop cryin'."

I dabbed my eyes again, and he walked closer to me. "Is this why you don't want to take our relationship to the next level?" I asked.

"Next level? Fuck you talkin' about, Elite?"

"I'm talking about marriage! You putting a ring on this finger and making me your wife."

He stood in front of me and pulled me to my feet. He let his arms rest around my waist as he looked into my eyes. "You already my wife. You know that."

I sucked my teeth. "Not in the eyes of the law, and you know it."

"Since when you give a fuck about the eyes of the law?"

"You know what I mean, French. Be real with me. Why don't you wanna get married? If you ain't fuckin' Corinne, then that must mean you still out here stickin' your dick in every bitch you see."

He rolled his eyes. "Aw hell, here you go with that shit again."

"I'm just saying, be honest!"

"Maybe I don't want to get married because my ass is in

the streets heavy right now. What you gon' do if some nigga catch me slippin', huh? I got two boys and a baby girl to look after, and if I die, then what? My kids won't be shit but lil' bastards."

"At least I will have a piece of you! Some stability!"

"So that's all this about? Having a piece of me?"

"It's deeper than that and you know it! Don't try to turn this around on me."

Frenchie lowered his head and let out an aggravated sigh. I gasped when he picked me up by my ass cheeks and held me suspended in the air. "You really get on my mothafuckin' nerves, Elite, you know that?"

"You get on my nerves too, nigga."

"You lucky I fuckin' love your ass," he said as he walked back toward the door and pinned my back to it.

He ran his hands over my ass and then grabbed my pussy. My body jolted forward, and my lips landed on his. Frenchie quickly stuck his tongue inside my mouth. He pulled my T-shirt up over my ass while fumbling with his belt. He licked his fingertips and slid the wetness of them between my thighs, then pushed his wide dick inside me. I pulled in air through my teeth as my walls tightened around his dick.

I held the sides of his face and gazed into his chocolate brown eyes. Frenchie was everything I wanted wrapped in everything I didn't need. With my back pinned against the door, he wrapped his strong hand around my throat and bounced my petite body up and down on his dick.

"Mmm, shit," I moaned in his ear.

He buried his face in the crevice of my neck and kissed all the way down to the tip of my shoulder. "You love me?" he asked.

"Yes, Frenchie, I love you!"

He gripped my waist and started thrusting upwards, going balls deep inside me. As brutal as it sounded, it felt heavenly.

"You gon' marry a nigga, Elite?"

"Mmm, yes, baby!"

"You gon' be my wife?"

"Yessss! Mmm, fuck!" I squealed, digging my nails into his shoulder blades. "Don't fuckin' stop, baby. I'm about to cum."

Frenchie dug his nails into my ass cheeks, pumping harder and faster to bring us both to our peaks. Seconds after I came, I knew he was right behind me.

"Fuck," he groaned as he released his warm cream inside of me.

As soon as we caught our breaths, there was a tiny knock on the door. "Mommy? Daddy?"

"Yes, baby?" I called.

"Daddy's friend Rico is here."

"Damnit, Mani, what did I tell you about opening the door without my permission?" I said, opening the door to scold her.

She lowered her eyes. "Sorry, Mommy."

"It's okay, baby girl," Frenchie said, picking her up. "Let's go downstairs."

SAVANNAH

My body sprang forward when my phone started ringing loudly beside my head. With my heart nearly beating out of my chest, I quickly grabbed the phone and answered.

"H-hello?" I answered, clearing my throat.

"Good morning, McKinney. How are you feeling?"

"Good morning, Chief. I'm doing much better."

"I was just calling to let you know that Agent Shepard and I will be over in a few hours to talk next steps for Operation November."

I nodded as I flipped the covers off my body. "Yeah, sure. That'll be great. I'll be here."

"Okay. See you later."

As soon as I hung up, I fell back against the pillow and looked at the time. It was a quarter past nine. Pharaoh and I had stayed up half the night talking, and I didn't get much sleep. Warm air blew out of my nostrils as I peeled myself away from the bed and went into the bathroom. The moment I splashed cold water on my face, my eyes fully opened and memories from the night before with Pharaoh flooded my brain. He was a beautiful creature. If his lips were any preface to what the rest of his body felt like, I was in for one hell of a ride if that day ever came.

THERE WAS A hard knock on my door almost three hours later. I hurried over and let the chief and Agent Shepard inside.

"It's been a few weeks. How are you feeling?"

I nodded with a smile. "I'm good. I'm really good."

"What about your therapy sessions?"

"Yes, sir. I've been calling in twice a week, just like the doctor told me to."

"Good. As I mentioned on the phone with you earlier, I brought Agent Shepard here with me today to go over the details of everything with you again. I've informed him about your memory loss."

"Okay. Nice to meet you... again, I suppose."

"Yeah, again."

I nodded and sat on the couch. "So, what's up?"

I watched Agent Shepard as he stood across from me, looking out of my window at the view. "I've been undercover for almost six and a half months now. I know they are looking for a new connect, and that's where you come in. I'm going to set up a meeting between you and Frances's cousin. You're going to meet in the back of a Japanese restaurant downtown."

"Why Japanese?"

"They have a close relationship with the owner. I just found out they run their drug money through a bunch of different businesses in the city."

"Okay, so I go and meet, and then what?" I asked.

"You tell them you want to talk business. He won't be expecting a female, but you are going to show him that you know your shit."

"How?"

"Offer him a few hundred pounds of marijuana as a sign of good faith just to see if he takes the bait. As much as he's going to want to call your bluff, don't let him. We have to bait him in with the cheap drugs before he'll take you seriously with the hardcore shit," Shepard told me.

"Okay."

"I'll be there with him whenever I can set it up, and when you come, I'll make sure you have two undercover agents with you as your bodyguards in case anything goes down."

"It feels like a setup," I told them.

"It is," the chief said.

"Weren't you the one who told me this guy was smart? He's not going to fall for any of this. If you want to bait someone, why don't we bait his cousin? You've already caught him once, right?"

Shepard nodded. "She's right, and he's fresh out of jail, too. I know he's hungry and ready to get back to makin' some money."

"Exactly. The cousin is the weaker link. Let's feed off it while we can," I said.

He nodded again. "Okay, I'll talk to him and try to get in his head. Whenever I can get the meeting set up, just remember they know me as Rico, not Michael or Shep."

My face screwed up in confusion. "What did you just say?"

"They know me as Rico."

I stood up from the couch and walked over to the kitchen.

"Are you okay?" the chief asked me.

"Uh, yeah, yeah, I'm fine."

"Are you sure?"

I looked at them both and nodded. "I'm good. Set it up. I'm in."

Chapter Eight

FRENCHIE

"Ooh fuck! Fuck, yes, Frenchie! Right there!" Corinne moaned as I dug her pussy out from behind like I was trying to give her my fourth child.

She kept squeezing her nipples while I fucked her and smacked her juicy ass. Rin had always had the phattest ass in the city. She had the type of ass to make a nigga go weak in the knees anytime she walked past. I knew what I was doing was going against my relationship with Elite and the family we shared, but it was what it was. She knew I was a dog ass nigga when I met her. Just because I suppressed the bark didn't mean I could stop my tail from wagging in another bitch's direction every now and then.

I slid my dick out of her, and she snapped her neck around to look back at me. "Nigga, what the fuck you stop for?" She pouted.

"Show me what that mouth do besides talk," I said, grabbing my dick.

I reached back onto the nightstand and grabbed the creased one-hundred-dollar bill and lifted it up to my nose. I sniffed a line of coke while I watched her get on her knees to suck me off. "Hit this shit," I told her.

She took the bill and sprinkled some of the powder onto my shaft and sniffed it off. "Mmm, fuck! That's some good shit."

"That shit was sexy as fuck," I told her as I gripped the

back of her weave, forcing her to deep throat my shit.

Rin wrapped both hands around it and slurped and sucked my shit like it was the last dick piece of she'd ever get in her life. "Mmm, shit, mama; keep suckin' daddy dick just like that."

I could feel my toes curling inside my socks. I loved hearing her gargle on my shit while watching her play with her pussy. My phone vibrated in my pants pocket on the floor, and I darted my attention down to it.

"You wanna answer that?"

"Fuck that phone, Rin. Keep suckin'."

She continued to suck me off until I came in her mouth, and she swallowed it. As much as I wanted to lay up and take a nap, I backed away from her and swiped my shirt off the floor to put it back on. "Aight, I'm about to head out."

"You leavin'? For what? I thought you was gon' stay until Junior came home from school."

"You know I can't do that. I got shit to handle. The only reason I came over this mothafucka was to bring you money for Junior's winter jacket and to tell your ass to chill on the textin' and shit. Elite went through my fuckin' phone again."

She rolled her eyes. "Oh, so she's the reason you over here bitchin' up on me. I get it now."

I pulled my pants up and fastened them, then dug in my pocket and pulled out two one-hundred-dollar bills from my stack. "Here. This the last time I'm givin' you shit until I know it's goin' to some real shit."

"Nigga, fuck you! I don't need your money!"

"Then why the fuck you keep askin' me for it then? Huh?"

She rolled her eyes. "Why the fuck you always gotta run back to Elite? She don't own you."

"Because she's my woman. C'mon now, Corinne. We been through this shit I don't know how many fuckin' times."

"Don't try and play me, nigga! I know all your dirty little secrets. Don't pull the petty out of me, because once it's out, I'll fuck around and blow up your whole life," she said like the bitter bitch I knew she was.

"Just remember, you blow my shit up and yours will collapse right along with it. Don't be fuckin' stupid, Rin."

I tossed the bills on the bed and left her ass sittin' there.

PHARAOH

Ever since I'd kissed Savannah, I didn't want anybody's lips on mine but hers. It was getting harder for me to restrain myself when I was around her, but if I had it my way, I'd see her all day, every day if I could. The phone rang three times before I heard her voice on the other end.

"Hello?"

"What are you wearing right now?"

She burst out laughing. "I'm sorry, what?"

I chuckled. "Just tell me."

"Hmm, I have on a pair of black Adidas sweatpants, an oversized white T-shirt, and some fuzzy socks."

"I wanna see you."

"When?"

"Now."

"Ugh." She groaned. "Now I have to change out of all this comfortable stuff just to look presentable for you."

"Nah, leave your sweatpants on, I don't care. I just want to see you... And there's something I want to show you."

"What is it?"

"Just be ready in thirty minutes. I'm about to pull up on you."

As soon as she hopped in my ride, I took her to my favorite spot downtown. We pulled up to the hotel with the words "The Drake" illuminated in bright purple neon lights on the top of the hotel. Once we got out, I let the valet park my car, and we headed inside. I led us up to the top floor and into my deluxe suite for the night.

"We're here," I said as I held the door open for her.

She walked in and looked around. "Why'd you bring me up here?"

"This is one of my favorite views of downtown. I thought you'd appreciate it with your bangin' ass view and all."

"I do. It's beautiful, it really is. But be real with me..."

"About what?"

"It's almost ten o'clock at night... We're in this nice ass hotel suite, and you mean to tell me you ain't bring me here to try and fuck?"

I walked over to her. "You wanna know the truth?"

"Yeah, I do."

"I got a lil' crush on you, that's all."

"A crush, huh?"

"Yeah, that's what I said... and I wanted the opportunity to do this again."

I lifted her chin up to kiss her soft lips, making sure I pulled away after a few seconds. As much as I wanted to explore her body, I wasn't gon' force anything on her that she wasn't ready for. Pussy was thrown my way every day. I knew how to chill and wait for what I wanted.

"You gotta stop doin' that."

"What I do?"

"Makin' my knees buckle and shit." She giggled.

I smiled and sat on the sofa, then propped my feet up on the coffee table. "Come here."

She waltzed over to me and plopped down beside me, throwing her legs onto my lap. I slid her shoes off one by one and grabbed her left foot.

"What are you doing?"

"You want this foot massage or not?"

"I'm not complaining, I was just asking. Please, carry on." She smiled.

SAVANNAH

I watched Pharaoh closely as he gently massaged my feet. "Mmm," I moaned and quickly slapped my hand over my lips. "I am so sorry. Oh my God! **Please excuse me while I go die of embarrassment!**"

"Nah, you good. I kinda liked that shit."

I smiled and rolled my eyes at him at the same time. "I bet

you did."

Pharaoh went back to massaging my feet, and I rested my head against the plush fabric of the couch. His phone vibrated, and he stopped to pull it out of his pocket. He looked at the screen and then turned it upside down and put it on the table in front of us.

"Are you sure you don't want to get that?"

"Nah, it was just my nigga Rico. I'll hit him back later. Right now, I'm spendin' time with you."

The wheels inside of my head started turning, and a wave of uncertainty coursed through my veins. "Um, how long have you known Rico?"

He shrugged. "A while now. He proved his loyalty to me when he saved my life."

"How'd he do that?"

"Long story short, I was out one night at the club. Some nigga's girl tried to push up on me, and he got mad. I told him it wasn't my fault he couldn't control his bitch, and his ass tried to bust a bottle over my head. That mothafuckin' Rico stopped him, pulled him out of the club and *BOW!* Put a bullet right in that nigga's head."

My eyes widened. "He what?"

"Yeah, been down with his ass ever since."

"Wow... That's really intense. And you said he just came back from Atlanta because his grandma passed away?"

"What's with the sudden interest in my boy?" he asked with his eyebrow raised.

"Nothing... It's nothing."

"It don't sound like nothin'."

I shrugged it off. "What can I say? I'm a woman, and I'm nosy sometimes. I'm sorry if it came off pushy."

"I think I know a way that I can take your mind off it."

"Oh yeah? How?"

Pharaoh smiled, pulled me on top of him, and kissed me. I instantly melted inside his arms. "You are too much for me," I whispered as I slowly pulled away.

"What do you mean?"

"You're making me feel things... lots of things that I haven't felt in a long time."

He pushed my hair out of my face and stared deep into my eyes. "Tell me how you really feel then."

I quickly shook my head. "It's not that easy to put into words."

He rubbed my shoulders and let his hands slide down my arms. "Try."

I sighed. "I don't know... It's like ever since you crossed my path, things have been different. I've been different, but in a good way."

"I've been different too."

The room fell silent, and I was stuck listening to my hormones run amuck inside my body. "Let's listen to some music... It's too quiet in here, and my thoughts are extremely loud right now."

"Play whatever you want."

I climbed off his lap, grabbed my phone, and went to the R&B station on my Pandora app. As soon as my body flopped back against the couch, Pharaoh leaned into me.

He lifted my shirt, and I pulled at them hem of his, running my hand along the rippling muscles of his back. His big, powerful hands pressed against my waist as he pulled me underneath his lean, powerful body. Everything between us was snowballing into something much more. I was already in too deep, and I didn't want him to stop. I wanted him in every way humanly possible.

Pharaoh pulled his shirt over his head and started kissing on my neck and down to my chest. "Trip" by Ella Mai came on, and I froze. My eyes popped open, and I stared up at the ceiling. Within seconds, everything came flooding to the forefront of my mind.

"I remember," I whispered.

"What?" he asked, looking up at me.

I pushed him off me and sat up on my elbows to look into his eyes. "The crash… the fire… everything."

"Are you okay?"

There was a growing lump in my throat as he looked at me. "I'm sorry. I—I can't do this."

"What's wrong?"

"I have to go. I have to go home right now."

"Savannah, chill. Just tell me what's wrong."

"I can't. I'm sorry. I have to go."

I climbed off the sofa and scurried out of the room, leaving Pharaoh shirtless with a confused look on his face. As soon as the elevator doors closed behind me, I rested my head against the wall. Everything from the crash, the trip to Atlanta, and my acceptance of the new job came flooding back all at once. The man I'd fallen for was the man I'd signed up to take to jail for life.

"Oh my God, what have I done?"

Chapter Nine

ELITE

I was upstairs, getting ready for work, when the doorbell rang. I ran downstairs while putting the other hoop earring in my ear and opened the door to see Rico standing there.

"What's up, Elite? Is French here?"

"No, he left about an hour ago. What's up?"

"Nah, I needed to holla at him for a second about somethin', that's all."

"Please, come in. You don't have to stand out there." Rico walked into the living room and stood by the couch. "Hey, um… can you do me a favor?"

"What is it?" he asked, looking at me.

"I need you to talk to French, please."

"About what? What's going on?"

"I think he's gotten into some shit he shouldn't have."

"Like what?"

"I found a hundred-dollar bill with white powder residue on it, inside his pocket."

He let his head drop toward his chest. "Damn."

"Yeah, damn is right. Will you talk to him, please?"

"What the fuck you want me to say to the nigga, Elite? I'm not his daddy. He ain't gon' listen to me. The only nigga he listens to is Pharaoh."

"I want it to be you. I know you're wrapped up in all this BBG shit, but I can see right through all of that."

"What do you mean?"

"I mean, I can tell that you're a good person, Rico. He needs someone like you in his life. We all do…"

He flashed his perfect smile at me, and I looked away. "Thanks, Elite."

"No problem. But will you talk to him for me? Please?" I asked, giving him my puppy dog eyes.

"Don't do that shit, Elite."

"Please?"

"Yeah, fine; I'll do it. I'll talk to him, but I'm not makin' no promises."

"Thank you so, so, so much, Rico. You don't know how much this means to me. I have to go down to the shop now and make sure them bitches ain't runnin' my business straight into the ground, but I'll see you later, and you can let me know what happened."

"Okay. Have a good day…"

I smiled at him. "You have a better one."

Rico watched me get inside my car and pull off before he pulled off. I wore a smile all the way into the shop. The moment my foot stepped over the threshold into my business, I locked eyes with my receptionist, who was standing up and arguing with a customer. I immediately put on my business voice and walked over to them.

"Excuse me, is there a problem here?" I asked.

The woman quickly snapped her neck around to me and rolled her eyes. "Good, you're here. You're just who I wanted to see."

I shook my head and let my business voice fly right out the window. "What the fuck are you doing here, Corinne?"

"I came to talk to you."

"About?"

She looked back at my receptionist as if to tell her to give us some privacy. I nodded. "It's okay, Nique. I got this."

"You sure? Because the bitch knows damn well her ass ain't welcomed in here," Nique snapped.

"It's fine. I got it. We're going to the back."

I led Corinne's big-headed ass down to the back of the shop where my office and all the supplies were. As soon as we got inside, I put my purse down on my desk, and she closed the door. "Speak."

She sucked her teeth. "I just wanna know where the fuck you get off tellin' French that he don't need to be givin' me no more money for our son. That's our business! Just because you livin' with the nigga don't give me the right to tell him how to raise his kids with you, so don't do that shit when it involves my son!"

"Look, all I told him was that he didn't need to be comin' over and givin' your ass cash when you never have anything to show for it! If you say Junior need a coat, then why can't you give him the size and we go out and buy him what he needs?"

"*We*? Bitch, please. You really thinkin' because the nigga sleep next to you every night that he's gon' marry your ass, don't you?"

"Corinne, when are you gon' let it go that you lost, sis? Frenchie loves me. He knows that, you know that, hell, everybody in the mothafuckin' Chi knows that."

"That may be the case, but that nigga got a long way to go before he ever does that, so don't pass out holdin' your breath, boo."

As much as I wanted to fight against the urge to ask what had been sitting on the tip of my tongue since I saw her, I cracked my lips open and asked anyway. "You're still fuckin' him, ain't you?"

"He was my man first, remember?"

I rolled my eyes and let out an aggravated sigh. "How many times do I have to tell your ass he ain't never say shit about you when I met him! There were bitches hanging all over him the night we met."

"And yet your thirsty ass still went for him, huh?"

Arguing with Corinne's hard-headed ass was a lost cause. She had no idea what transpired between French and I the night we met. I was a fresh twenty-one-year-old, celebrating my birthday with my girls the night I met Frenchie. He was the center of attention in the club with a bottle glued to his hand. My heartbeat quickened as soon as we laid eyes on each other from across the room. He had girls hanging all over him, but I didn't care. I wanted him, and I didn't know shit about him.

He walked over to me and leaned in to my ear. "What yo' fine ass celebratin' tonight?"

"It's my twenty-first birthday," I told him.

"That's what's up. Let me buy you a drink then. Hell, I'll buy your fine ass the entire fuckin' bar."

He bought me a drink and then invited me and my girls to his section, and I fell in love. In the blink of an eye, I became Frenchie Blackwell's girl, and I just knew shit was going to be sweet. That was until I found out that not only did he have a girl-friend at home, but a baby on the way with her, too. I wanted to walk away, run even. The same night I was going to break things off with French, I found out I was pregnant. I didn't know what I was going to do. We hadn't been together long enough, and he'd already proved himself to be a liar. But I was in love with him. He made me feel... everything. Good, bad, in between, being with Frenchie made me feel.

I snapped out of my trance when I heard Corinne mumble, "How you get them is how you lose them, remember that."

Corinne gave me the answer to my question in her dumb ass comeback. I already knew what was up. I just had to catch his ass in the act. She turned and walked out of my office, while I stood there with my blood boiling. Because of Frenchie's lies and infidelities, Corinne and I were sworn enemies for life. We shared children with the same man, but it sure as hell didn't make us friends.

DOING HAIR WAS my passion. I was a certified weave surgeon. All my clients left my shop laid to the gods. I spent the rest of my day tightening sew-ins, laying edges, and trying not to think about my run in with Corinne. Although I owned the shop, I knew my employees were lookin' at me and shaking their heads, while mumbling under their breath about how dumb I looked. They just had enough respect for me not to say it to my face. As soon as I finished my last client, Nique came over to my station.

"You good, E?" she asked, referring to Corinne's impromptu visit.

"Yeah, I'm good. Thanks for havin' my back this morning."

"Anytime. You know any enemy of yours is an enemy of mine."

I nodded. "Yeah, I know."

"What did that bitch want though?"

I sucked my teeth. "To tell me to stay out of whatever it is that has to do with her and Frenchie's son."

Her forehead creased as she folded her arms across her

chest. "What? Like he ain't about to be your stepson one day."

"Yeah, and she told me not to hold my breath on getting a ring. I should've said, like you were, bitch?"

"Exactly! You can still see the thirst in that hoe's eyes anytime she talks about him. She wants to be you, Elite, that's all."

"I know. I did ask her if she was still fuckin' him though."

"And? What she say?"

"She didn't give me a straight answer."

"Well, that's your answer right there," she said, shaking her head in disgust.

"I know…" I looked back at my station and started cleaning up. "Yo, you think you can run me somewhere?"

"Aww shit, what's up? I know that look."

"What look?" I asked.

"That, 'I'm about to fuck a bitch up' look. I have the same one," she joked.

"Yeah… somethin' just isn't—"

"Right in your spirit? Yeah, it's written all over your face. Where we goin', girl?"

"We gon' pull up at that bitch house and see what's up. I gotta see shit with my own eyes before comin' at Frenchie's neck again. He's never going to be man enough to tell me the truth."

"Let's lock up and go then," she told me.

I sat in the passenger seat of Nique's car as we pulled onto Corinne's street. She slowed the car down and flipped off the lights and then crept down some more. "Hold up. Ain't that Frenchie's car right there?" she asked.

I looked up and then lowered my eyes. "Yup, that's him."

Before showing up, I didn't know if French had a faithful bone in his body. Two kids later, and I still wasn't enough for him. I was worn to the bone, and I was done.

"What are you gon' do, girl?" she asked while glancing over at me.

I could feel the tears filling up in the back of my eyes. "I don't know."

"I mean, we can be like me and pull up and go right up to that bitch mothafuckin' front door and show our asses, or we can be more like you, and chill and think rational and shit."

"I wanna wait for him to come out."

"Okay. Well shit, I'ma pull up right behind that nigga's car then."

Nique parked right behind Frenchie's car and rolled down her windows. "You mind if I smoke? Shit like this gets my nerves jumpin', and I need to calm down before a bitch go to the trunk, you feel me?"

"It's fine. Do what you gotta do," I said with my eyes glued to Corinne's front door.

"You sure you alright, girl?" she asked.

"I'll be alright."

"Today was crazy, like… first that bitch showed up, and then the shop was crazy packed!"

"Did anybody talk about it?"

"Talk about what?"

"You ain't gotta lie to me. I know the girls at the shop be talkin' shit 'bout me. I used to be the same way."

"I mean, they do, but it's not shade. Everybody just knows you deserve better, and we want you to have that."

"I have two kids with that nigga, Nique. It's just not so easy to get up and leave…"

"You just gotta want it bad enough. You don't want it yet. You're still too in love."

I nodded while brushing a tear from the corner of my eye. "I can't believe I really thought after all the shit he put me through that I would still get my happily ever after."

"You still could get it, just maybe not with him."

"What nigga you know gon' want a bitch with two kids and a crazy ass baby daddy?"

She shrugged while puffing her blunt. "Girl, you'd be surprised."

My eyes widened when I saw Corinne's front door open. She wasn't wearing anything but a matching bra and panty set. He pulled money out of his pocket and stuffed a few bills in her bra. I glanced over at Nique, who had already taken her seat belt off and had her hand on the handle to get out of the car.

"Stay here, Nique! I got this!"

As soon as he made his way across the street, I jumped out of the car. "So this is how you do me, nigga?" I yelled as I ran up on him and swung at him.

He quickly grabbed my arms and pushed me back against the hood of his car. "Yo, Elite, chill! What the fuck is you on right now?"

"What the fuck am I on? Nigga, what the fuck are you doin'? Out here disrespectin' me by fuckin' with your whore ass baby mama!"

I glanced over at Nique, who had half of her body hanging out of the car, ready for me to say the word. Before I knew it, Corinne came out of the house wearing a silk robe and a smile.

"Oh hey, Elite. Still holdin' your breath, huh, sis?" She cackled.

"Go the fuck back in the house, Rin!"

"Yeah, go the fuck back in the house before I black your shit!" Nique yelled.

"See what the fuck you did!" French yelled at me.

"Me? Nigga, we all in this mess because you can't keep your mothafuckin' dick in your pants!"

"I ain't come here to fuck her."

"Yeah, like I believe that shit," I said while rolling my eyes.

"If you shut the fuck up once in a while then maybe you'd let me tell you that I just came here to drop off some money for Junior's field trip next week."

"And some dick, too, right?"

Frenchie sucked his teeth. "That's your problem. Always talking when you should be fucking listening."

"Fuck you, French! I don't give a fuck what you say you were over here for. I know what the fuck I saw! I'm not stupid! I'm done with all of this shit!" I yelled, throwing my hands up in the air.

His forehead creased. "Done? Where you gon' go?"

"Yeah, I'm done! I'm leaving, and I'm taking the kids. You can't keep putting me through this shit, walkin' all over me like I'm nothing when I give you everything, Frenchie! I give you everything and more!"

"Tell him, girl!" Nique yelled.

"Tell your mah'fuckin' friend to go home before I bust her loud ass upside her head."

"She'll leave when your thot ass baby mama go back in the house!" I yelled.

"Who you callin' a thot?" Corinne yelled, stepping closer.

Frenchie stepped in front of me and grilled Corinne. "Go the fuck back in the house, Rin. I'm not gon' say it again. I got this."

"Yeah, you better handle her," she said, rolling her neck.

I watched her sashay back into the house and then turned to Nique, who was standing by her trunk with the lid open. I shook my head at her, and she closed it. "I got this, Nique. You can go."

"You sure you don't want me to stay?"

"Nah, we good," Frenchie answered for me.

"I'll call you," I told her.

We watched her get in the car and pull off. As soon as we saw her brake lights flash at the end of the street, Frenchie turned back to me.

"Now just hold up a second, Elite. You trippin' right now, for real."

"I'm trippin', nigga? No! You're trippin'! You been trippin'! If you think I'm gonna sit here and continue to waste my best years on a nigga who clearly don't want me, you're wrong."

"So you already got another nigga on standby is what you sayin'?"

"That's not what I said at all, but if I did, why the fuck would you care?"

Frenchie stepped up to me and grabbed my throat. "Listen to this, you ain't goin' no fuckin' where. My kids ain't goin' no-where. You know why? Because if you leave me, I'll kill you!" he said, followed by a kiss on my lips.

I pushed him away from me and shook my head. "You're crazy."

"Crazy in love with you, Elite," he joked.

"You think this shit is funny, nigga? You can't see the pain you're causing me?" My voice cracked as tears immediately came flooding out of my eyes.

His face went stiff. "I know, and I'm going to fix it, I promise."

"Fix it how? You can't fix this!"

"Look, Elite. I know I fuck up a lot, and I know you don't deserve that shit. Just know that I'm tryna spend the rest of my days on this earth with you. Please, stop cryin'. You know I hate seein' you do that shit."

I wiped the tears from my eyes. "I don't know what that means, Frenchie. What are you saying?"

Frenchie stepped back and rested his weight on his back foot while looking down at the ground. He looked up at me and flashed his perfect smile while running his hands down his beard.

"Marry a nigga."

"What?"

"You heard me, Elite."

I sucked my teeth. It was far from the proposal I thought I'd get. "How you want me to marry you with no ring? I should've known that everything that comes out that stupid mouth of yours is bullshit. You only askin' me to marry you now because I finally got your ass shook. You ain't foolin' nobody; you just wastin' more time."

"Get in the car."

"No!"

"I said get in the mothafuckin' car. I'll show you how serious I am. We goin' straight to the jewelry store right now, and you can pick out the biggest, brightest diamond you want."

My forehead creased. As much as I knew he was full of shit, I wasn't about to call his bluff for a second time. Without saying another word, I got in the car and put my seat belt on. I knew deep down he felt the only way to keep me in his life was to step up and ask for my hand in marriage. I knew a diamond wouldn't stop all his bullshit, but at least it would give me more stability and a better status in the streets so I could keep the hoes at bay.

PHARAOH

I looked at myself in the mirror as I slid on a black blazer over my white button up. My phone vibrated and then illuminated. It'd been days, and I still hadn't heard a word from Savannah. As much as it fucked with me, I pushed past those thoughts and grabbed my shit to head to Big City's funeral.

The last time I stepped foot in a church was to bury my grandmother. I never liked the way being in them made me feel. I'd done too much dirt to ever be fully cleansed by the blood of Jesus. I parked my car and dapped up Frenchie as soon as I got out.

"What's good, fam?" he asked.

"Shit. How you doin'?" I asked.

He shook his head while pulling his pre-rolled blunt out from behind his ear, then felt around in his pockets. "Shit, you got a lighter, nigga?"

I nodded and pulled one out of my pocket to hand to him. He lit his blunt, took a hit, and then passed it to me. Normally, I would've probably told his ass no, but I didn't want to feel shit. I took it from him and hit it a couple times, then passed it back.

"Let's head into the church."

"Yo, come over to the house after all this shit is over. We havin' a kickback at the crib for Big City. His family and all the BBG niggas is gon' be there."

I nodded. "Bet."

LATER THAT NIGHT, I was sitting in French's living room with a swig of liquor left in my cup and another blunt in my hand. Frenchie came out of the kitchen with a bottle of Hennessy in his hand and Elite right on his heels.

"Yo, turn the mah'fuckin' music down for a second. I wanna say something!" he yelled.

Once the volume was lower, he looked around at all of us. "Yo, we are all here tonight to celebrate the life of our nigga, our hitta, Big City. That nigga was a real one."

"Wasn't nobody realer!" someone shouted out from the crowd.

"Hell yeah, wasn't nobody mah'fuckin' realer. So I want everybody in this bitch to lift your cup in the air. This one is for my nigga Big City; may he always rest in peace," he said, while pouring a bit of his liquor onto the carpet.

Everyone raised their cups and took whatever they had inside to the head.

"Aight, and now that we got that shit out the way, my baby and I have something to say. You wanna do the honors, baby?"

Elite nodded and then looked around. "We're gettin' married!" she yelled.

Everyone cheered, clapped, and sipped some more, while I got up to dap up my cousin for finally doing right by Elite. As happy as I was for them, it made me think about Savannah and why I hadn't heard from her even more.

"Yo, congratulations, my nigga," I said, pulling French into a hug.

"Thank you, nigga."

"It's about time!"

He shrugged. "I know. A nigga had to grow up one day, right?"

"I'm proud of you, fam."

"Thank you." He smiled.

"I'ma step outside real quick. I'll be back," I told him.

I stepped outside onto the front porch and pulled out my phone to call her. As soon as I put it up to my ear, it went straight to voicemail. I had half a mind to go over to her spot and see her in person, but I didn't want to come off as a stalker nigga. Although I'd already claimed her as mine, we weren't together. If she didn't want to talk to me, then I just had to play the background and do me until she did.

I slid my phone back in my pocket and then the door opened. Some female came outside with a bottle of D'USSÉ attached to her hand. "You look like you could use a drink," she told me.

I looked down at my empty cup and nodded. "Pour me up then."

She poured some more liquor into my cup, and I threw some of it back, then held my cup out for more.

"Oh, you tryna get fucked up, fucked up, huh?" She giggled.

"Somethin' like that," I told her.

She poured some more into the cup and then shook her empty bottle at me. "Looks like I'm all out."

"That's too bad," I told her.

"I got some more... back at my house. I live like two streets over if you wanted to slide through..."

I looked up from my cup long enough to give her a once-over. She had a cocoa brown skin complexion with low eyes, and her juicy lips glossed. Her blue eyebrows matched the long blue weave in her head. She had a slim waist and an ass that was just as juicy as her glossy lips. As tempting as she looked, I shook my head. She wasn't who I wanted.

"Nah, I'ma pass."

She stepped closer to me and ran her long, pointed nail down the side of my face. "You sure about that? I'm sure we can have a really great rest of our night together."

"You ain't even bother to tell me your name yet, but you cool with me comin' to where you lay your head? You wild reckless."

"I tell you what I want you to know, nigga. Damn, as good as I look, you'd think it wouldn't be this hard to get some good dick!"

She sucked her teeth at me and pushed past Riot to get back into the house just as he'd stepped outside. He laughed and looked at me. "Yo, what's up?"

"Ain't shit up. What you mean?"

"I mean, I know I came out here a little late, but it look like she was tryna give you a nice lil' night cap, if you know what I mean."

"And?"

"And? The Pharaoh I know wouldn't have thought twice about slidin' up in some new pussy."

"Nigga, are you gettin' me confused with you?"

He looked at me and then burst out laughing. "Yeah, nigga, you prolly right. I forgot you all boujee with your shit."

"Yeah, just mind your business, nigga."

"Damn, nigga. I was joking. What's good with you? You got your face all twisted up and shit."

"Nah, I'm good. I am about to head out though."

"Where you goin'?" French asked as he joined the two of us outside.

I threw the rest of my drink back and looked over at him. He had a hundred-dollar bill in his hand and was sniffing a thin line of coke off it. My forehead scrunched up, and I almost smacked that shit out of his hand. "Nigga, what the fuck are you doin'? Is this a thing now?"

"Chill. I'm just tryna relax and have a good time."

"Elite know you on that shit?"

"I ain't on it; I just hit a bump every now and then. It's been a stressful day, mothafucka! Damn!"

I shook my head. French was already a crazy ass nigga. He didn't need shit else in his system to make him crazier. Rico walked outside before I stepped off the porch. He had a red solo cup in his hand and a cigarette behind his ear. "Damn, nigga, I've been lookin' for you," he said.

"What's up?"

"You about to leave?"

"Yeah, why?"

"You think you could drop me off somewhere?"

"Yeah, whatever, nigga; let's go."

We dapped everybody up and then got in my car. The moment Rico sat his ass down on my leather seats, I looked over at him. "Yo, did you know about French and the white girl?"

He lowered his head. "Nah, not until recently. I came by to talk to him not too long ago and Elite brought it up to me. She wants me to talk to him about it."

"You?"

"Yeah, that's exactly what I said. I told her he ain't gon' listen to a word I say, but I told her I'd try anyway. I just didn't think tonight was the right place or time."

"French is a hard-headed ass nigga," I said as I pressed the button to start the engine. "Where am I takin' you to anyway?"

"It's not too far from here; I'll show you where to go."

I nodded and started driving. Rico gave me turn-by-turn directions until I started to realize the direction we were going. He wanted me to drop him off at Savannah's apartment complex. "Yo, who you know that live over here?"

"Just some girl I met." He shrugged.

I tore my eyes away from the road and glanced at him. "She got a name?"

"Yeah, she do. Why?"

"Nah, I'm not tryna be all up in your business or nothin', I just know somebody who stay over here too."

"Just wanna make sure we not fuckin' on the same bitch, huh?" he asked with a chuckle.

"Yeah, somethin' like that," I said as I pulled up.

Rico dapped me up and then got out of the car. "Thanks for the ride, my nigga."

I slowly nodded in his direction and watched him go up to the door, punch in a code, and walk into the building. My eyes darted over to the clock on the dash. It was 1:32 a.m. I pulled out my cell phone one more time and called Savannah's number. Within seconds of connecting, it went straight to voicemail. An exasperated sigh blew past my nostrils as I put the car in drive and sped down the road. I sure as hell hoped he wasn't goin' to Savannah's apartment for both their sakes.

Chapter Ten

SAVANNAH

Almost an entire week went by, and I ignored every text and phone call from Pharaoh. I was still so shaken up over my memory coming back that I didn't know what to do. I jumped at the sound of the knock on my front door and scurried over to look through the peephole before opening the door for Shep.

"It's about time you got here."

"I was out. What's the big emergency?" he asked.

"You smell like you were out, but whatever. Come in, come in."

"What was the big rush that I had to get over here tonight?"

I walked into the living room and flopped down on the couch. "All this time I've been getting these tiny bits and pieces of my memory, and then one night, everything hit me like a ton of fuckin' bricks."

He sat on the arm of the couch beside me. "What do you remember?"

"Everything. I remember every fuckin' thing. The crash... the fire... everything."

"Okay, that's a good thing though, right?"

I shook my head. "Not in this case."

"Why not?" he asked with confusion written all over his face.

I huffed and dropped my head in my hands. "I met this guy while I was in the hospital... And we hit it off."

"Okay, and? I'm still not seeing the problem here."

"It was Pharaoh Blackwell," I mumbled.

I looked up at him in time to see his eyes widen. "What?" he asked.

I jumped off the couch. "I need to leave. I need to get the fuck out of Chicago now. Tonight!"

"Just calm down. Does he know where you live?"

"Yes, he's been here!"

"Fuck! And I just got that mothafucka to drop me off here!"

"You what?"

"Nah, I didn't tell him who you were. I just told him I was comin' to see some girl. But now that explains it."

My forehead creased. "Explains what?"

"Why the hell he was askin' me so many questions when we pulled up."

"What did he ask?"

"Asked your name and just said he knew someone who stays here. Wait... Are you fucking him, Savannah?"

"No."

"When's the last time you talked to him?"

"I haven't. I've been avoiding him ever since my memory fully came back. I don't know what to even say to him."

"Look, if he finds out who you really are and what you really came here to do, he'll kill you or even worse, he'll kill both of us. You need to call him and apologize. You need to stay in Chicago."

"Stay? Are you kidding me? No. I can't stay like this. Not after all I've done and what I know."

Shep stood to his feet and grabbed me by my shoulders to keep me from pacing the floor. "Take your heart out of your panties, McKinney, and remember why you came here in the first place."

I took a long, deep breath and closed my eyes. "You're right."

"You know this changes everything now, right? We're going to need an entirely different game plan."

"I know, but if I have to do it, then let me do it my way."

He eyed me closely, checking for any reservation in my tone or body language. "Are you sure you're going to be able to do this, Savannah?"

I chewed my bottom lip while slowly bobbing my head up and down. "I don't have a choice. Just promise me you won't tell the chief about any of this. I feel like he already looks at me as a liability."

"I won't. This will stay between you and me," he assured me.

WHEN I WOKE up the next morning, I nervously picked up my phone and called Pharaoh. The phone only rang twice before I heard him answer.

"Hello? Savannah?"

"Hey... Yeah. It's me."

"What type of shit you been on?"

I cringed at the sound of aggravation in his voice and sighed. "Look, I know you want answers."

"Hell yeah I do. Why the fuck you ain't hit me? I didn't know if you were hurt or what. You just ran out that mothafucka freaked out like you saw a ghost. I really had to sit back and question myself, like what the fuck did I do to make this girl so uncomfortable?"

"I know… No, it wasn't you, it was me, I promise. It's just… Things were getting real hot and heavy really fast, and I just needed some air."

"A week's worth of air?"

I blew out the air I was holding in my cheeks. "I have really big lungs." I chuckled. The phone went silent, and my heartrate quickened. "H-hello?"

"Yeah."

"Not buyin' it, huh?"

"Nah."

"That's fair. How about we talk about it over dinner at my place… if you're down," I suggested.

"What's on the menu? S'mores again?" he joked.

I laughed. "No. What's your favorite thing to eat? Whatever it is, I'll make that."

"Something with fresh lobster in it."

I frowned. "On second thought… we can just order in."

He chuckled. "Aight. I'll see you later then."

By the time Pharaoh got to my front door, I already had the food plated and waiting. He walked in and looked around. "It smells good in here."

"You can thank the Japanese take-out restaurant down the street for that." I shrugged.

"What exactly did you order?"

"Shrimp and scallop hibachi for myself and seafood hibachi for you, which has shrimp, crab, scallops, and lobster in it."

"Nice."

"Would you like a glass of wine or something?"

"You tryna get me drunk so I'll forget how you played me?" he asked.

I lowered my head. "I knew that was coming. And again, I'm sorry. I really am."

"Tell me what happened then."

I sighed and took a seat at the dining room table by my plate. "You remember I told you about my celibacy?"

He nodded. "Yeah, and?"

"Like I told you earlier, things just got really heavy that night, and I got scared..."

"I scare you now?"

"No, not you. It... sex... intimacy. I just wasn't sure if I wanted to go there with you, so I froze up, and I left. I just needed some time to get my head together because I was freaking out; that's all, I promise."

The hard look on his face softened, and he cracked a slight smile. "As long as things are okay now. I ain't gon' lie. You scared me."

"Scared you? How?"

"I thought once I told you I had a crush on you, you dipped out on a nigga." He chuckled.

I smiled. "No, that wasn't it at all. I thought for sure after this, you wouldn't want me."

"Nah, I still do."

I let out a sharp breath and flashed my eyes up at him. "Then why haven't you kissed me yet?"

Pharaoh stepped closer to me and pulled me out of my seat. The moment he placed his lips on mine, I felt electricity coursing through the soles of my feet up to the hair follicles on the top of my head. His tongue swirled around my mouth as he ran his strong hands down the small of my back, stopping to palm my ass. We both slowly pulled away from each other and leaned our foreheads together. The both of us were out of breath after such a long kiss.

"Damn, Savannah."

"I know, right."

We stared at each other in silence. I could see the hunger in his eyes as he stared at me. "Fuck dinner. Tell me I can have you now."

My eyes bore into his soul. I couldn't see the monster I'd read or heard about. All I could see was the man that made my panties wet every time he looked at me. He was nothing but a stupid man with brown eyes. I didn't know why I was more addicted to him than I could be to any drug, but I needed Pharaoh. I craved him.

"Can I have you, Savannah?" His lips asked the question that my body was dying to answer.

"Yes," I said, waiting breathlessly for his reply.

Pharaoh's lips took possession of mine, and my body instantly flushed with heat. I could've kissed him forever. I drew his tongue into my mouth and gently sucked on it. The two of us couldn't have stopped if we wanted to. I melted into his arms as he scooped me up and carried me into my bedroom and laid me down.

His fingertips slid underneath my shirt and grazed my bra. He slowly lifted my shirt up over my head and unhooked my bra. I slowly slid the straps down and tossed it to the floor. Pharaoh flicked his tongue as he sucked on my nipples.

"Mmm," I moaned breathlessly.

He let his fingertips race down to the front of my jeans and unbutton them. I quickly shimmied from side to side to get them down around my ankles so that I could kick them off to the side. Pharaoh licked his two fingers and slowly slid them inside of me while sucking my hard nipples.

The tightness of my sweet spot gripped his long fingers, and I felt his dick pulse against my thigh.

"Just relax," he whispered.

I let my head sink into the pillow as I closed my eyes. Instantly, I felt his hands touching me everywhere. His fingertips glided across my oversensitive skin, which sent chills through my body.

He kissed my heart. "I plan to get to know you inside and out tonight."

"I'm sure you might find some imperfections along the way."

He shook his head. "Nah, you're already perfect to me."

Pharaoh spread my legs from east to west and trailed open-mouthed kisses on my inner thigh. He gently slid my thong to the side and kissed my pussy. I slid my bottom lip in between my teeth and tried to clench my thighs together when his tongue dipped in between the seam of my lower lips.

"Ahh, shit," I moaned.

His strong arms pulled my thong off and pried my legs apart with ease, while he made deep sweeping strokes against my clit with his skilled tongue. His mouth explored the folds of my flower, making the number eight over and over and over again. The tips of my nails pinched my nipples as I tossed my head back against the pillow. "Mmm, shit."

I had an unyielding grip on the back of his head, forcing him to stay in position. Pharaoh wrapped his hand around my neck and licked harder, faster, sloppier.

"Oh fuck! Fuck! Yess! Oh my God, right there!"

My wide hips bucked forward, yearning to feel the mesmerizing electric jolt through my body. My thighs tightened around his neck as he drove me right to ecstasy. He slid his large hands underneath my ass and then sat up. I could see the hardness of his dick pressing right through his jeans.

"Take your clothes off," I told him, ignoring what any of my actions would mean when the sun came up the next morning. *'Fuck it,'* I told myself. I was living in the moment.

Pharaoh's lips parted, revealing a glimpse of his white teeth. He stepped back slowly, never breaking eye contact with me. He ripped off his shirt and tossed it on the floor, then undid his belt and let his jeans drop slowly to the ground. My teeth sunk into my bottom lip as I watched him with desire seeping through my pores.

I sat up on my knees and stared his hard dick in the face. My tongue lured the head of his dick into my mouth. I sucked lightly on the tip while my fingertips ran up and down his thighs. He tightened his grip against the back of my head as I slowly licked from his balls all the way up to the shaft to get it nice and wet.

He stepped back, and I watched him reach into his jean pocket and pull out a condom. Once he put it on, Pharaoh tossed me back against the bed, lifted my right leg over his shoulder, and pushed his hard dick past my tight walls. My breath hitched as the fine hairs on the back of my neck stood on end. A small breathless whisper escaped my lips as I bit down on my bottom lip.

"Open your eyes and look at me," he demanded.

My eyes slowly cracked open, and I stared at the finely sculpted muscles of his chest as they tightened with every stroke. His body crashed against mine like ocean waves as he kissed me gently then increased the pressure. My legs wrapped around his waist as I dug my nails into his back, scraping his honey brown skin. Pharaoh buried his head in the nape of my neck while kissing my neck.

When our lips found each other again, I curled my lips around his tongue, sucking on it slowly. He growled in my mouth and pressed his weight into me harder. My fingertips clung to his broad shoulders as his hard chest grazed my nipples in a steady rhythm.

"Mmm, fuck," I whispered.

I could feel a pool of moisture underneath me as millions of tiny fireworks exploded throughout my core. My back arched as continuous light moans burst past my lips.

"You don't always have to be in control, you know?" I purred as I pushed him off me and then straddled his dick.

I slowly slid down on top of his length and started gently grinding against it. My body was savoring every minute of Pharaoh's being inside me. Our bodies moved simultaneously like one pulse, one heartbeat.

"Shhhiiit," he groaned while gripping my waist tighter.

"Mmm," I moaned as I kissed from his earlobe down to his neck.

"You better stop ridin' me this good unless you want me to give you my seed tonight, Savannah," he growled into my ear.

My body quivered at the sound of his baritone voice. I froze, relinquishing the power back to him. Pharaoh's grip on my waist tightened as he began to jackhammer his dick inside me. "Oooh my fuc—fuckin' God," I squealed.

"Turn over," he demanded while smacking my ass.

Pharaoh bent me over so that my face was in the pillow, spread my ass cheeks, ran his tongue in between them, and then entered me from behind.

"Oh shit," I moaned.

He ran his thumb down my spine while smacking my ass. My eyes rolled back in my head as my bouncing nipples grazed the sheets. I reached back and spread my ass cheeks apart so he could go deeper, all while keeping up with the cadence of his stroke. I could feel myself beginning to cum all over again.

"Yes, Pharaoh! Right there! Don't stop!"

Pharaoh's hand rested on the small of my back while he pumped into me. He was giving me the A-1 dick that I needed, and my body was aching to cum again. He pulled me by my hair so that my back would straighten out. With his chest pressed to my back, he kissed my neck while wrapping his hand around to stroke my clit.

"Yeah, that's it right there, ain't it?" he growled in my ear.

"Mmm, fuck! Yes!"

The powerful thrust of his thighs mixing with the warmth of his breath on the back of my neck sent me flying over the edge one last time. After a few more deep strokes, Pharaoh's grip around my waist tightened and his body jerked calmly. Our sweat-drenched bodies collapsed on the bed as one as we both tried to catch our breaths.

"Is it weird that I wish we could stay like this forever?" I asked as I reached up and ran my fingers through my messy sex hair.

"Nah. At this point, I don't think I could stay away from you if I wanted to."

"Why not?"

He shrugged. "I don't know how to put that shit into words."

"Just try."

He lifted his shoulders and quickly let them fall. "I don't know... I guess you make me a better nigga."

I sat up on my elbows and looked at him so hard it was as if I could see through him.

"What?" he asked as he leaned down to kiss my hand.

"I can see the demons in you, Pharaoh, but I also see so much more than that. And that's what scares me the most."

"What do you mean?"

I sighed as I fully sat up and wrapped myself in the covers. "I thought if I just follow the rules and stayed down that everything would be fine, but you had to come along and knock me off my square."

"That's what happens when you start fuckin' with a real one, Savannah. You'll never meet another nigga like me in your life."

"I'm betting on that," I said, flashing a smile at him.

"I'm betting on you," he told me and kissed my lips.

He pulled me on top of his lap and kissed me deeper. He slowly slid the cover off my breasts and began sucking on my nipples again. "See, you about to get somethin' started again," I moaned.

"I'm betting on that, too." He smiled.

ONE WEEK LATER, I was standing next to Shep in front of our chief in an undisclosed location.

"Got anything for me?"

I lowered my head. "Um, no sir. Not yet, but I firmly belie—"

"What do you mean no? You mean to tell me you two still haven't set up the meeting with his cousin yet? What about you, Shep? You got anything for me?"

"He's been utilizing a storage unit to store kilos of cocaine."

"You got the address?"

"Yeah, it's located at 390 South Wabash Avenue. There have also been members of the gang who have been traveling to Texas on a monthly basis and trafficking anywhere from fifteen to twenty kilos of cocaine from an undisclosed source."

"Good work, Shep. You're free to go. McKinney, I want you to stay back."

"Okay, sir."

Once Shep closed the door behind him, I turned my attention back to the chief. "Sit down," he told me.

"No, sir. I'm okay to stand."

"I said put your ass in the chair!"

I chewed my bottom lip as I let out a calming sigh before taking my seat.

"Listen to me, McKinney. If we don't get a handle on this shit and wrap it up with a cute fuckin' bow on it, DEA special agents are going to swoop right in and steal all this shit right from underneath us, you hear me?"

"Yes, sir."

"Good. I want Blackwell's head on a platter by the end of the month, if not sooner. If you don't think you can give me that, then bow out now and turn in your badge."

"I understand, sir. I'll make sure we get that meeting set up as soon as possible."

"Go on, get outta here."

Shep was waiting for me outside. As soon as I saw him, I rolled my eyes.

"What he say?" he asked.

"What you think he said?"

"That bad, huh? At least he didn't say it in front of me. That would've been more embarrassing."

I sighed. "How do you do it?"

"Do what?"

"Separate reality from… whatever we're doing with Pharaoh and his people. I mean… I used to be able to turn it off and on with the snap of a finger, but ever since the plane crash and then losing my memory, only to regain it… shit has been ten times harder."

"Nobody is asking you to be perfect, Savannah."

I scoffed. "Tell that to the chief. Hey, um... how'd you know about the storage unit? He's never mentioned that before. Well, to be honest, we never talk about that side of him or what he does. It's just assumptions."

"It's not assumptions when you know the truth."

I nodded. "Yeah, I know...we just...he's not who he seems to be on paper. You spend just as much time with him as do. You know there's good in him, right?"

"You're not going to want to hear this, but I'm going to tell you anyway. I think you're too close to him. He's blinding you. The moment you realized who he was, you should've taken a giant leap backwards."

"I did! I tried to bow out and go home, remember? You are the one who told me to stay in it!"

He rolled his eyes. "I know that, and I'm sorry. I thought that it may be easier if you got to him on a personal level, instead of the business level that we were originally going to go with, but now I see that he's keepin' you in the dark because he cares about you, too. This is a fuckin' scary game you're playing."

I nodded. "I know. I fuckin' know."

He sighed. "Look, Savannah. I like you and all, but... your heart is getting in the way of your ability to do your job effectively, and I know you know it too. It's always duty before love, never the other way around. Facts are facts, okay? Prison was made for people like him, and it's people like you and me who make sure we put him there."

I turned away from him and cast my gaze down to my shoes. He was right. If I was sane, there would be no competition between my heart and my mind. Pharaoh Blackwell would've already been behind bars, and I could've moved on with my life.

But instead, I was playing with the idea of possibly falling in love with him. It terrified me what I was willing to do for Pharaoh, solely because of how I felt about him.

"You make it sound so easy," I told him.

"It can be, if you let it. Some people just aren't worth saving, Savannah."

I shook my head. "Don't you get it, Shep? It's too late! I'm knee-deep in my feelings with the three letters on my back that make me the ultimate target!"

"He's already got his claws sunk into you too deep."

I remained silent, too afraid to tell him that I'd fallen in love with the sharp, piercing feeling.

"Look, you do what you gotta do, but I'm gonna let you know this. I'm gon' talk to Frances and the moment I get a recording of his ass sayin' anything in reference to the drugs, the murder, the gang shit, anything. I'm blowin' the fuckin' whistle, and I'm taking this shit down whether you're standing by my side in the end or not."

"I'll be there. I'll break the law if I have to," I told him.

"In favor of who? Your job or for him? He's your target, not your man, remember that."

I could feel myself getting frustrated. I didn't need him laying on more shame. I had given myself enough to last for a lifetime. "I know what I'm doing, Shep!"

"Do you? Because I'm really starting to think otherwise! You're in too deep, Savannah. Is this how you want it to go down? Is this how you want it to end for you? Your career? Your life?"

I sighed, not wanting to add more fuel to the fire. "Trust me, I got this."

"Just make sure you don't bring us all down with you," he said and left me standing there alone.

Chapter Eleven

FRENCHIE

"Yo, Elite, go on and get the door!" I yelled from the bathroom.

"Nigga, why can't you get the door?"

"Because I'm in the fuckin' bathroom, takin' a shit!"

I heard her smack her lips and stomp down the stairs like she was ten years old. I loved Elite's crazy ass, but she was too much for me at times. Always askin' more of a nigga when I was doin' the best I could. I knew I wasn't perfect, but she saw past that shit. She'd been there when I had it all and when I didn't have shit to give her but babies and broken promises. That's why I allowed her to hold onto my heart. She stuck with my ass when no other bitch would.

I went downstairs and saw Elite and Rico talking. Usually, I wouldn't have thought shit about it, but the way her ass was smilin' in his face while she was wearin' my ring made me feel some type of way. "Yo, am I interruptin' somethin'?" I asked, stepping in between the two of them.

"What? Boy, bye," Elite said as she walked into the kitchen.

"Yo, Rico. Can you step outside for a second? I need to holla at Elite real quick."

He nodded and stepped outside. Once the door closed, I walked into the kitchen and looked at Elite. "What the fuck was that shit about, Elite? You smilin' in another nigga's face while you wearin' the diamond that I bought you?"

"What the fuck are you talkin' about?"

"You supposed to be my bitch."

"Bitch? First of all, nigga, I ain't nobody's bitch, aight? You better watch who the fuck you talkin' to, ring or not."

I shook my head. "You know what I meant, Elite."

"No, nigga, I know what you said!"

"All I'm sayin' is, you're bein' too friendly with the nigga."

"Ain't that what friends do? Be friendly?"

"Nah, that nigga been lookin' in your direction a little bit too long to just want to be your friend. This ain't the first time I seen that nigga lookin' at you either. I'm about to go check his ass."

"Calm your ass down, Frenchie! You said it yourself, I'm yours, I got your ring. Stop trippin'."

"Yeah, well next time, act like you mine then."

"Mm hmm, bye," she said, waving me away.

I walked out of the kitchen and outside to the porch. Rico was sitting on the steps, and I sat beside him. "So what's up, nigga?"

He glanced down at me as soon as I started lighting my blunt. I hit it two times and then passed it to him. "So, I got a business opportunity for us," he said.

"Business opportunity? Fuck you mean?"

"What if I told you we could get twice the amount of drugs we're bringin' in now for a lower price."

My eyebrows knitted in confusion. "I'd tell you you're dreamin', nigga. That shit only happens in movies and urban fiction novels."

"Nah, nigga. Believe it. I've been tryin' to put this shit together for a while now, and it's finally starting to come together. I just need you to have my back on this and go with me to meet them."

"Why me?"

"What you mean?"

"I mean, why didn't you go to P about this shit?"

"I've tried. I've been callin' this nigga for the past few days, and his ass ain't pickin' up."

"He's been ignorin' your shit, too?"

"Yeah. He doin' the same to you?"

I nodded. "Yeah."

"What the fuck is up with that nigga?"

"What you think? He got himself a new bitch. He got a girl, now the nigga gettin' soft."

"Look, fuck all that. I'm just trying to see what's up with the money. If he ain't gon' do it, then we can't just sit here twiddlin' our fuckin' thumbs, right?"

I cut my eyes at him and then nodded. "Yeah, you right. Set that shit up. We'll see what they talkin' about and then decide if it's worth tellin' P about."

"Bet." He nodded. "Oh um, before I go, can I holla at you about somethin' else?"

"What up, nigga?"

"At the kickback at your crib for Big City, I saw you fuckin' with the Miley Cyrus. What's up with that shit? That's your thing now, nigga?"

"Nah, it ain't. I just be doin' it to unwind and shit. A nigga been stressin' out, my nigga."

"About what?"

"I don't know. I just got a bad feelin' about shit ever since that nigga Big City died. I can't shake the shit."

"Hey, but at least you getting married, right? And we about to get to this money, nigga, so that ain't nothin' to stress about, right?"

I nodded. That nigga Rico always did have a way to try and brighten the mood and shit. When Pharaoh first brought his ass around, I didn't fuck with him. I could never wrap my head around why a random nigga would save another nigga's life when it ain't have shit to do with him. Nobody I knew did shit for nothing, and I knew there would come a time where Rico's ass needed somethin'.

"But yeah, I'm about to get out of here. I'll holla at you later."

I nodded. "Aight, bet."

I watched him pull off from the street corner and drive

down the street. I puffed the last of my blunt and made myself a mental note to keep an eye on that nigga.

ELITE

As soon as Frenchie made his way back into the house, he walked up behind me in the kitchen and kissed me on the neck.

I brushed him off. "Stop, French."

He sucked his teeth. "Don't tell me you still mad about that shit, Elite."

"And if I am? That's my business, not yours."

"You actin' up. You want some dick, baby? I can prescribe you some," he growled in my ear as he pressed his growing erection against my ass.

Before I had a chance to say anything, he propped me up on the countertop, pulled my shorts to the side, and started swiping his tongue against my pussy.

I slowly pushed his head away and hopped down. "No, stop, nigga, for real."

"What the fuck is wrong with you?" he asked while wiping his lips on his hand.

"This! This is wrong with me," I said, holding up a crinkled hundred-dollar bill with more white residue on it. "What the fuck are you doing, Frenchie?"

He sucked his teeth. "Why the fuck is everybody talkin' to me about what I do like I'm a fuckin' child? First Rico, now you?

What the fuck, Elite? Is that why you were over there smilin' all in that nigga's face, so you can tell him my business?"

I rolled my eyes. "Okay, yes, I did ask him to ask you what the fuck was going on. What the fuck else do you expect me to do? We have two kids now, Frenchie! You're supposed to sell the shit, not use the shit! Fuck is wrong with you?" I yelled.

"Your ass is the reason I do the shit! Always on my mothafuckin' back about what the fuck I'm doin', or who the fuck you think I'm fuckin'. You drivin' me fuckin' crazy!"

"This is a joke, right? This has got to be a mothafuckin' joke! After all I do for you, I should be the one sniffin' fuckin' coke, not you! You got it easy, nigga!"

"You don't trust me enough to know what's good or bad from me? I'm a grown ass man, Elite. You over there pillow talkin' with the next nigga about what the fuck I'm doin' is crazy to me. That's like lettin' that nigga in my mothafuckin' bed."

My blood was boiling. Frenchie wouldn't last a day in my shoes. If I did half the shit to him that he did to me, he would've killed me years ago. Feeling defeated, I shook my head as I looked at him with tears in my eyes. "Can't you pretend to love me? Just once? Is your ego really that big?"

His forehead creased in anger. "Man fuck this shit, I'm leavin'. Save that bitchin' you doin' for somebody else."

"What the fuck is up with you callin' me a bitch, nigga?" I said, swinging at his face.

He caught my hands and shoved me back toward the refrigerator. "Keep your mothafuckin' hands off me!"

Frenchie turned around and started walking in the opposite direction. "If you walk out this door, then we're done!" I yelled at his back.

He cut his eyes at me when he reached the front door. "Then I'm done."

The door slammed, my heart broke, and the baby started crying all at the same time. With warm tears streaming down my eyes, I slid my dream engagement ring off my finger and tossed it across the room. I wiped my tears as I walked over to the bassinet and picked up my son. "Shh, it's okay, Pax. Mommy's here."

PAXTON AND IMANI had both been asleep for hours when I decided that if I was going to be in my feelings, I at least wanted to be knee-deep in a bottle of wine. I flipped through channels and picked up my phone when I got an Instagram notification. I went into the app and opened the message from a female I'd never seen before. My eyes widened as I read her message from left to right. I quickly slammed my eyes shut as my heartrate quickened and my hand began to tremble. I tossed the phone to the side and slowly picked up my glass of wine. The moment I took my first sip, there was a knock on the door. I wiped the tears from my stinging eyes as I swung the door open to see Rico standing there.

"Yo, is French here?"

"Nah, he ain't here."

"Damn, aight… Um, you okay?"

I shrugged. "Yeah, I'm good."

"You sure?"

"I said I'm good, Rico. Just drop the shit."

He threw his hands up in surrender. "Okay, okay. I was just checking. Do you uh, do you know when he's comin' back?"

"He's not," I said while batting away fresh tears.

His eyes widened, and his lips twisted to the side. "I'll leave if you want me to."

"As much as I don't want you here, I don't want to be alone either. The kids are asleep, and I'm just up trying to dig myself out of my feelings."

"Do you want to talk about it?" he asked, still standing in the doorway.

I shrugged and then took a step back. "Wanna come in and find out?"

He pressed his lips together and came inside. I closed the door behind me and pressed my back against it. "Before I start, promise me you won't tell him about this. Don't tell anyone."

"Your secrets are safe with me, Elite," he assured me.

My face went blank, and I rested the back of my head against the door. "It's getting too hard to keep pretending like everything is okay all the time. I thought us getting engaged meant that we were going in the right direction, but that diamond wasn't shit but a pacifier until the next time he fucks up."

"What brought all this on?"

"Now I got a bitch tellin' me that my man, my fiancé, is the father of her unborn child. She's five fuckin' months. Do the math. How old is Paxton? I'd be a fuckin' fool to stay with him after all this, but it's like my feet want to move, but my heart is stuck in cement," I vented.

Rico lowered his head. "Damn."

"You think I'm crazy, don't you?"

He chuckled. "Nah, not at all. I think it's kinda cute when you get angry."

I twisted my lips into a quick smirk. "Thanks... You know, there are some times when I wish I could forget I ever met him, but then I wouldn't have my kids."

"I know what I'm about to say is going to sound crazy, and it goes against everything I believe in as a man, but I just gotta say that nigga Frenchie don't deserve you, Elite. No disrespect to your heart, but you deserve so much more than what that nigga gives to you. There's a whole world outside of this small ass city. Find you a nigga that can give you that shit."

My eyes never broke away from his lips as he talked. The longer he spoke, irrational thoughts filled my head, one right after the next. I knew Rico hadn't been around that long, but I could tell he was a sweetheart, even if he rarely ever smiled. Besides that, his perfectly straightened teeth and sexy beard were just some of his desirable qualities.

I shrugged. "I just need a hug sometimes. A nigga that'll tell me to have a great day. Open the door for me once in a while. Pick up after himself and wash his own funky ass socks. Is that too much to ask for?"

"Nah. If you ask me, you not askin' for enough."

I smiled, and he flashed one back at me. I knew I should've never been pillow talking with the next nigga, but I couldn't help myself. Rico made me feel so comfortable in the matter of a few minutes. "You just sayin' that."

"I have no reason to lie to you. I'm just sayin', you need a nigga that makes you feel something in between those thick ass thighs when you hear his name."

I instantly clenched my thighs together, which sent a tingle to my sweet spot. "Wow."

I looked up at him and caught his gaze. "If I didn't know any better, I would swear you were flirting with me."

"If I was, is it working?"

"Maybe, but I think it might be time for you to go."

He nodded. "Yeah, you're right."

"Goodnight, and thanks for listenin' to my problems."

"Not a problem. Goodnight," he said as he reached out to hug me.

His chest pressed against mine, and I sunk into him. "Wow."

"What?"

"You are ridiculously comfortable. I think you are like the best human pillow ever." I chuckled as I ran my fingertips down his sides.

"You know what I think?"

"What?"

"You're beautiful," he whispered in my ear.

"Rico, I'm flattered, but…" I said, trying to pull away.

He held my waist tighter. "Wait, don't pull away… not yet. You said you wanted a nigga that could hug you, right? Just enjoy the moment."

I sighed and lowered my gaze. The last thing I wanted to do was look up at him. Although I felt awkward, a part of me wished I could skip ahead just to see what would happen next. I loosened my muscles and rested my ear against his heartbeat. It felt so good to genuinely be wrapped in someone's arms and not waiting for the other shoe to drop.

"You never did tell me why you came by here to talk to French."

"To be honest, I didn't."

"Then what did you come here for?" I asked him.

He dropped his arms back down to his side and shot his gaze down to the floor. "When I was over here earlier, I heard French talkin' to you crazy about me, and I wanted to come here and apologize if me talkin' to you in front of him started anything."

"Nah, his insecurities go far beyond you or me," I assured him.

He gritted his teeth and let out an aggravated sigh. "You make me want things I can't have, and that shit is startin' to drive me crazy."

My heartbeat quickened. "Rico, I—I don't know what to say. Where is all this comin' from?"

"This ain't nothin' new. I been noticed you. I bet French has to fight niggas off you all the time."

"Nah, it's definitely more like the other way around," I said, chuckling at the irony of the situation.

"See, and that's the shit I'm talkin' about. I know I haven't known either of you that long, but I know you're a good woman. I care about you, and I just don't want to see you keep getting hurt."

"Care about me how?"

"Look, I got two older sisters, and I grew up watchin' niggas disrespectin' them, and I swore I would never treat any woman that way."

I looked at him like the rare specimen of a man that he was. "How are you even single?"

He shrugged. "I've never found a woman I felt was worth fighting for."

I nodded. "Oh."

"Until now," he said, eyeing me. "Just be honest with me.

If you were single and our situation was different, would I have a chance with you?"

I shifted my weight from one leg to the other. "Rico, you seem like a good guy and all, but—"

"Say no more," he said, cutting me off.

"Wait, let me finish."

"Nah, I don't wanna hear that 'you nice, but' shit. It don't matter how nice I am. You're not ready to stop breaking your back for him."

My forehead creased. "Why would you say somethin' like that after all I just shared with you?"

"Then let me show you what bein' with a real man is like, Elite."

I quickly shook my head. "It will never be that easy."

He turned to leave. "When you stop being afraid, holla at me."

"I'm not afraid. I just—"

"Then let me kiss you right now."

Rico wrapped his hands around my waist and gently kissed my forehead. I slightly pulled back and looked up at him. "Something tells me I'm going to regret you."

"Shh, no regrets," he whispered against my lips.

The moment his lips touched mine, a spark went off inside my chest. Rico slowly slid his tongue inside my mouth as his hands slowly glided down the small of my back and over my ass. I felt cool tingles slowly spread through my body and quickly shot my eyes open. "Oh my God! What the fuck am I doing? My kids are upstairs," I said, pushing him away from me.

I wiped my lips and walked halfway to the other side of the room to put as much distance in between us as possible. I pushed my hair out of my face and then ran my palms down my cheeks.

"Elite, I—"

"You need to go."

"I'm sorry, if I—"

"Now! Please go!"

Rico turned to leave and closed the door behind him. I couldn't believe I pillow talked right into the arms of a nigga in Frenchie's inner circle. Nothing but trouble could come from it, and as much as I needed to stay away, I knew that moment would be etched in my mind for nights to come.

Chapter Twelve

PHARAOH

I tossed my hoodie over my head as I bobbed and weaved through traffic down the interstate. My phone started ringing through the car speakers, and I looked at the screen. Frenchie was calling, and I was going to ignore him and anybody else who dialed my number. As good as it felt to be around Savannah, I knew she was the type of woman I'd get lost in if I wasn't careful. I put my phone on 'Do Not Disturb' and turned my music up so loud that the bass vibrated my windshield.

The engine slowed down to a dull murmur as I put the car in park and got out. I grabbed the bouquet of flowers off the back seat and walked down to Big Mama's grave. I didn't visit as often as I knew I should've, but ironically, it was the one place in the city where I actually found peace.

I rested my back against the tombstone after laying the flowers in front. I closed my eyes and tried to put the millions of thoughts inside my head in order. The first thing that came to mind was Savannah. Although we hadn't known each other too long, I felt like I knew her in another life. I'd never been around a female who kept me on my toes and never expected anything from me. I had to make her mine.

After sitting in silence for twenty minutes, I got up and dusted off my pants. I never felt the need to actually talk to Big Mama. I always used our brief time together to get my head right before jumpin' back into my everyday life. As soon as I started my car back up, my phone illuminated. I glanced at the screen and noticed I had another missed call from Frenchie, so I called him back.

"Hello?" he answered.

"What you want, nigga?"

"Why the fuck your ass never answer the phone no more?"

"Nigga, I was busy. Fuck you want?"

"Busy bein' somebody bitch. You ain't gotta lie to me, nigga. I know when somebody got your attention. You've been walkin' around with your nose wide open."

I sucked my teeth. "Fuck is you tryna say?"

"How well do you even know this girl?"

"Fuck is what I'm doin' any of your business?" I asked, raising my voice.

"You know what, fuck it. You a grown ass man. You do what you gotta do."

"So that's what the fuck you were blowin' up my shit for? To tell me I'm actin' like a new nigga?"

"Nah, to be honest, I was just going to ask your ass if you were still havin' everybody over to your spot or not."

"Yeah," I said in a dry tone.

"Aight, I'll see you later then."

LATER THAT NIGHT, I opened the door for Savannah, welcoming her to my kickback. I pulled her into my arms and kissed her cheek. My nostrils drew in her scent, and I licked my lips. "You always smell so fuckin' good," I whispered in her ear.

She smiled and gently pushed me away. "Stop. What are you sippin' on?" she asked, looking into my cup.

"Dark."

"Yuck. I'm not feelin' dark tonight."

"There's more liquor in the kitchen."

"Well then, I'm going to head into the kitchen and raid whatever bottles of liquor you have in there. I'll catch up with you in a second."

"Aight, don't take too long. There's someone I want you to meet."

She put a few feet of distance in between us, and Frenchie walked over to me. "So that's her, huh?"

"Yeah, that's her. I want you to meet her."

"Meet her? Fuck is you two about to do, go off to prom or somethin', nigga?"

I twisted my mouth up. "Just shut up and say hello when she come back."

"I'll meet her, but I meant what I said earlier, nigga. Watch her."

"Watch what?" Savannah asked, making her way over to us with a cup in her hand.

"Nothin'. Savannah, this is my cousin Frenchie. French, this is Savannah."

He looked her up and down then took a sip from his cup. "So you're the girl that got my cousin's nose wide open and ignorin' phone calls and shit."

She shrugged. "Guilty."

"Ah shit, that's what's up though. I'm glad to see my family happy. You just make sure he stay that way, aight?"

She nodded. "I'll do my best."

Frenchie looked across the party and turned to look back at me. "Yo, I'll holla at you later."

I took a sip of my drink and watched her babysit hers. "You don't like your drink?"

"No, it's not that. I just want to pace myself."

"Pace yourself for what? You with me, and you ain't got shit to worry about. Just relax and enjoy the night with your man."

"Oh, so we're doin' titles now?" she asked, looking into my eyes with her eyebrow raised.

I threw my arm around her shoulder and kissed her cheek.

"As far as I'm concerned, you been my girl since the moment I sent you them flowers in the hospital."

"Humph, nice to know." She smiled and then kissed my lips.

I grabbed her hand and led her through the sea of people. When we stepped outside, I wrapped my hands around her eyes from behind, and she froze. "What's going on?"

"I want to show you something."

"What is it?"

I pivoted her body in the perfect direction to see the lights light up on the brand new, winter white Range Rover that was pulled up in my driveway. I let my hands fall to the side and pulled the keys out of my pocket to press the button. The second the car lit up, her eyes did too.

"Damn!" she squealed.

"You like it?" I asked her.

"Like it? It's the most beautiful thing I've ever seen!" She beamed.

I chuckled and handed her the keys. "Here."

"What?"

"Take the keys. It's yours."

Her eyes widened as she looked down at the keys in her hand. "Pharaoh, are you fuckin' serious right now?"

"Yeah. Can't no woman of mine be gettin' rides with strangers to get around my city."

The light in her eyes slowly started to fade, and she handed the keys back to me. "I love it, I do. I just... I can't accept this."

"You can't, or you won't?" I asked her.

"A little bit of both." She shrugged.

"At least hold onto the keys in case you change your mind."

She smiled then kissed my cheek. "I won't."

"Do it anyway."

"You know what I will do?" she purred.

"What?"

"I'll let you fuck me in it."

I cracked a devious smile at her and wrapped my hands around her waist. "Let's go."

ELITE

The moment I saw Frenchie walkin' my way, I turned on my heels and walked down the hallway. He pushed his way through to me and wrapped his arms around my waist. "Why you walk away from me, girl? I know you saw me comin'," he said as he buried his lips into the nape of my neck.

I spun around and looked at him. He glanced down at my left hand and immediately acknowledged my bare ring finger. "Why you ain't wearin' your ring? You out here actin' brand new like I won't take you upstairs and break your back like I know you want me to."

"No thank you," I said as I tried to push past him.

He leaned into me, and I pressed my back against the wall. He rested his palms against the wall to stop me from leaving him standing there alone. "Stop playin' with me, Elite. I miss you, girl," he said as he kissed my neck.

I closed my eyes and felt the last piece of my heart break. There was so much regret trapped inside of me that I didn't know what to do. Rico was a great man, but I would always be Frenchie's girl in some shape or form, come hell or high water. I pushed his chest off mine and pulled my phone out of my purse. "You know what I got a few days ago?"

"What?"

"A DM on Instagram from a bitch tellin' me she been ridin' your dick every night for the past six months."

He sucked his teeth and rolled his eyes at the same time. "Aww, here we go with that shit again. How the fuck I been fuckin' her every night when half the time I'm layin' next to your ass?"

"Fuck the technicalities. The point is you shouldn't be stickin' your dick inside no other bitch, period!"

I shoved the phone in his face and he looked at her pictures. The second I saw the look on his face, I knew he'd fucked her. His lips could lie all they wanted, but his eyes never could.

"I know the bitch, aight? Damn, is that what the fuck you wanna hear?"

"So you admit it."

"Admit what? That I fucked her? Yeah, probably."

"You're admitting the fact that you got a mothafuckin' 'maybe baby' out here with this bitch?"

His eyes widened, and he shook his head. "Hold up. That bitch ain't never tell me about no kid."

"She said she's five months pregnant with twins, which would mean that you were fucking this bitch while I was pregnant with your child," I said, digging my nail into his chest.

He lowered his head. "Look, Elite, baby. Listen to me."

"No, French. I'm done."

"No, for real, just listen to me. Hear me out, okay? That's not me. That's not how I'm out here doin' shit. Yeah, I fucked her a few times, but I never dipped in that bitch raw. I swear to God that hoe is lyin', and that's on my kids. Those kids are not on me."

I screwed up my face as I wiped a tear from the corner of my eye. "Is this what it's gonna be like being your wife, Frenchie?"

He let out an aggravated sigh. "I don't know why the fuck you're so pressed to be my wife. As far as I'm concerned, you are already my wife. That marriage shit ain't nothin' but a piece of paper. It don't mean shit."

"Stop saying marriage is just a piece of paper. So is money, but you still get your ass up every fuckin' day and work for that shit, don't you? Don't deny me of this!"

I'd finally realized that the love I wanted and needed was no longer being served at the table, and I needed to get up. I had to stop going out of my way for a nigga who had started treating me like I was in the way, and I was spent on allowing him to love me with one foot in the door and one foot out.

"Sometimes I think this shit excites your ass, Elite. I swear to God it's like you love the fuckin' dramatics. You wanna hate me, but you love me. You wanna tell me I can't fuck you when I want to, like you don't want me to break your back like no other nigga could. I'm a fucked-up nigga, baby. That's what you signed up for. I'm who you love. I'm who you have two kids by. I'm who you want, flaws and all."

"So because you have flaws, I'm supposed to be okay with this shit that you call love? I swear to God you make loving you so goddamn hard. It's like another full-time job, and my heart can't take this shit anymore, Frenchie."

His forehead creased as he shook his head. "What the fuck are you sayin', E?"

"Read between the lines, nigga! I'm done with your ass! Through!" I said, sliding the engagement ring out of my purse and into his front pocket.

The moment I walked away, all the regret I felt instantly dissolved. From that moment forward, I was going to do me for the sake of my kids and my heart.

LATER THAT NIGHT, I found myself in front of Rico's front door. Being with him for the split moment that I was, awakened something inside me, and like a true fiend, I was coming back for more. He cracked open the door and looked me up and down. "Elite? What are you doing here?"

"You left Pharaoh's house early before I got a chance to

catch up with you."

"Yeah, I had somethin' to handle."

"Do you have company or somethin'?"

He looked back inside his apartment and then looked back at me. "Actually, I do. Is there somethin' you wanted to talk to me about?"

Feeling embarrassed, I quickly shook my head. "No, not at all. I just um, wanted to apologize for goin' ghost on you like I did."

"Does Frenchie know you're here?"

"I'm a grown ass woman."
"So, I take it that means no."
"Look, I'm sorry, okay? I was crazy vulnerable that night, and I freaked out."
"I get it. You ain't gotta explain shit to me. Emotions are never black and white, but in this case, they are. Either you fuckin' with me or you not, and clearly you not."
"What if I am?" I asked.
He chewed his bottom lip and then licked them. "Come in then."
I folded my arms across my chest. "I'll wait until you tell your company to leave."

"Ain't nobody in here but me."

"But you said—"

"I know what I said. I lied. I just wanted to see how you'd react."

I walked past Rico, and he grabbed my arm. He pinned my back against the front door and ran his fingers through my hair. "Tell me you feel this," he said.

He placed my hand over his heartbeat, while he slid his hand over my pussy to feel its pulsating beat. Our bodies were in sync. There was a blistering heat between our bodies as we both stood there, waiting for the other to make the first move.

He moved his hands over the nape of my neck and pressed his forehead to mine. "Tell me what you need, Elite, and I got you."

"I need you to fuck me tonight, Rico."

Heat rose between my legs as the words slipped off my tongue one by one. It was like watching Alice fall into the rabbit hole, but instead, I was falling into everything about him. Rico placed his lips on mine while sliding his hand up my dress.

"No panties, huh?"

"Nope," I whispered.

I meant what I said. Every nerve in my body wanted him to fuck me. I was jonesing for him in every way humanly possible.

"Perfect. Lemme taste you."

He took my hand in his, and I followed his footsteps over to the kitchen. He wrapped his arms around my waist, and an overwhelming tingling sensation gripped my body. He lifted me on top of the countertop and inserted himself between my legs. His lips claimed mine, and air could no longer escape my lungs. His kisses were filled with passion. He was kissing me in a way that I'd never been kissed before.

I held my breath as his fingertips traced the top of my thighs. His warm touch made my heartrate quicken. I ran my tongue over my lips after his tongue-thrusting kiss ended.

"Elite, you need to tell me if you want me to stop," he said, kissing my neck.

"No, don't."

He pulled my lips onto his once more and then dropped down to his knees. The second his tongue made contact with my flesh, goosebumps raised on my skin. My body was overflowing with emotion as he gently sucked on my clit. As much as I wanted him to stop, slow down, speed up, lick harder, anything, my body was paralyzed with pleasure from the waist down.

I sucked in air through my teeth and clawed the back of his head. "Oooh fuck!"

Rico gripped my ass and slid my pussy on and off his long tongue. I lifted my dress and pulled on my tingling nipples. He was tongue fucking me into another dimension. My chest tightened as I rolled my hips until I came. "Oh... my God," I choked out.

I took my hands off his head and watched him stand to his feet. He looked at me as he slid his hand down his wet beard. He leaned in to my ear. "You taste just like I thought you would. Sweet as sugar," he whispered.

I could feel the swollen thickness of his dick pressing against my inner thigh. He kissed me as I stroked his dick through his pants. Just the thought alone of his dick inside me almost sent me spiraling over the edge. My entire body ached with longing. He was going to make me beg for it. Rico's fingertips skated across the small of my back as he slid me to the edge of the countertop. My fingernails clawed down his hard chest and washboard abs, and I watched him slide inside me. My spine made a U-shape as he hit my g-spot with every single stroke.

"Oh my fuckinggg Goooddd," I moaned as loud as I could.

Each stroke took my breath away. Rico wrapped my hair around his wrist and whispered into my ear. "See, this is the type of dick you deserve. Every. Fuckin'. Night, Elite."

"Shiiiit!" I squealed as I locked eyes with him.

I wanted to lick every drop of sweat off his forehead, neck, and chest. I leaned forward, pressing a kiss to his chocolate brown chest. His front teeth sliced into his bottom lip as he stared at me. Electricity pulsed through my body as I felt myself on the brink of my climax.

"Yes, Rico! Right there! Right fuckin' there," I ached out.

The second I came, he slid my body off the countertop and fucked me all the way to his bedroom. By the time my head hit the sheets, I was cumming for the second time. Rico placed one hand on my thigh while the other was wrapped around my ankle.

"Tell me you love this shit," he demanded.

I nodded quickly. "I do. I really do."

The palms of my hands slid up and down his warm flesh as he looked into my eyes. "Fuck! You've unlocked something in me."

The sound of his raspy baritone voice growling in my ear sent waves of pleasure coursing through my body. Rico pinned my knees to my chest and dug me out so deep I could've fainted. I reached out and traced a line along his jawline with my index finger and then placed it inside his warm mouth. He sucked on my finger and then I reached down to massage my clit. Rico massaged my breasts through my bra as my eyes dripped tears of ecstasy.

"Shit," Rico groaned in delight.

I felt the anticipated tingling sensation coat my body as his strokes became harder and faster. He placed his lips on mine as he climaxed. He held his body tight to mine until the electricity between us faded. Once we caught our breaths, he slid out of me, and I pulled my dress down. Before I showed up at his doorstep, I thought Rico was just an itch I needed to scratch to feel better about getting back at French, but after hearing him say what he said to me and the way I felt when he was inside of me, I knew he was going to be so much more. I just didn't know if it would be in my lifetime.

I got off the bed and headed back toward the front door. "No one needs to know about this... aight?"

"I already told you, Elite. I'll keep all of your secrets."

Chapter Thirteen

FRENCHIE

It had been two weeks since Elite gave me back my engagement ring, and I was sick over it. Ever since I left the house, I'd been going from couch to couch. Some nights, I stayed with Corinne and Junior; other nights, I stayed at Pharaoh's crib or the bitch who claimed she was carrying my fourth and fifth seed. I hadn't seen or heard from her in months and she had the nerve to go to Elite about her pregnancy without talkin' to me first. Even though every bone in my body told me that they weren't my babies, I had to do what I had to do to secure a place to lay my head at night.

I woke up to Pharaoh making noise in his kitchen. He flipped the light on, and I squinted. "Yo, turn that shit off, nigga."

"Fuck you. This my house, remember?"

I sucked my teeth and rolled onto my stomach to block my eyes from the light.

"Nigga, wake your ass up. It's almost eleven in the morning. Fuck is you sleepin' on my couch so much for anyway?"

I sat up and buried my head in my hands to rub my eyes. "I think it's over between us for real."

"It ain't over, nigga. You know you and Elite break up at least once a week."

"Nah, this time is different. I snapped on her ass and told her I was done, then at your party she gave me back the engagement ring. I don't know what the fuck is wrong with me, nigga."

"You spiralin', and you need to catch yourself before you run out of thread."

Pharaoh had no idea what I was dealing with. My life

changed forever when Big City got killed. The bullets that pierced his chest were supposed to have been for me. I was tired of waitin' for P to put me back on once I got out of jail and decided to take matters into my own hands. I asked Big City to ride out with me that night. I had no idea what we were going to get into, but I knew it wasn't gon' be nothin' nice. I rolled up on an MCF nigga and put my gun to his head and told him to give me everything he had on him. Little did I know, I'd hit the jackpot. He only had a couple hundred dollars on him, but the keys to the car he was driving had two bags filled with cash and three kilos of coke in the trunk. Big City helped me get everything into my trunk, and right before we got back in the car to ride off with our come up, shots rang out. I sped off and left my nigga bleedin' to death on the cold Chicago sidewalks, and I'd never forgive myself for it.

"Yeah, I know I do," I told him.

"What's really up with you? This all can't be because you had a fight with your girl. I know you too well, nigga."

I shook my head. He was my family, but he didn't know me well enough. Nobody did. "I think Elite out here doin' a nigga dirty."

"What you mean? You think she fuckin' another nigga?"

"Yeah, I do. Shit has been too quiet. I try to talk, she don't talk back. I come and see the kids, and she goes upstairs and closes the door."

"Nah, man, not Elite. What in the fuck would make you think that?"

"I can feel that shit in my soul, nigga. That's real talk. A nigga know when his bi—I mean, his woman is steppin' out with another nigga. I mean, I know I ain't been the best to her and shit, but I ain't think it would come down to this."

His forehead wrinkled in confusion. "Come down to what? What you thinkin' about doin'?"

I shrugged and brushed the tip of my nose. "I gotta kill her."

Pharaoh's eyes widened. "Nigga, what the fuck did you

just say? Don't ever say no dumb ass shit like that around me ever again. You gon' kill the mother of your kids, for what? You just said you ain't been the best nigga to her, right? Then change that shit if you wanna get her back. She probably just fed up with your bullshit."

"I am who I am, nigga. That'll never change. You and I both know that."

An annoyed expression briefly crossed his face. "What happened to sucka free living, my nigga? Remember that? Don't let nobody's actions send you back on your third strike."

I shook my head, ready to change the subject and get my ass up from the hot seat before I said something I'd regret later. "What about you, nigga?"

"Me? What about me?"

"I know you, nigga! I also know that look. Just tell me what I already know."

"What?"

"You bit the forbidden fruit, didn't you?"

A sly grin slid across his mouth. "I don't know, man. It's just somethin' about her... pussy feels like home to a nigga, you know?"

"Hell yeah I do. That's why I know shit ain't right with Elite's ass."

"You say somethin' to her yet? Or you just gon' be over here plottin' for no reason?"

"Nah. Ain't no need. I already know what's up. I'm quiet, nigga. I'm not blind."

"I don't know why you sittin' here actin' like you don't love her, French. It's me you talkin' to, nigga."

"I do love her, but if you think I'm gon' sit up here and get played, then you got another thing comin'."

"Even after all the bullshit you done did to her? She held you down through the mud and everything, and you just gon' let

163

her go like that? That's crazy to me, but I ain't gon' tell you how to move."

My expression faded from reserved to serious. "That love shit ain't nothin' but a waste of time, nigga. Do yourself a favor and don't fall into that shit."

"When have you ever known me to be in love? I'm not in love with her, and she ain't in love with me either. We just... doin' what we gotta do, that's all."

"That's all, huh?" I asked, calling his bluff.

"Yeah, that's all." He cut his eyes at me, and I nodded. "I care about her and shit, but I can tell you that she's different."

"They all seem different at first."

"Nah, Savannah just... gives me something I can't go in my pocket and pay for."

I burst out laughing. "Aww hell, nigga. You actin' softer than a marshmallow right now."

"Speakin' of marshmallows, have you ever had a mah'fuckin' s'more, nigga?"

"What the fuck is a s'more? You got yourself a white girl? That sounds white as hell, nigga."

"Shut up. Don't knock that shit 'til you try it, aight?"

"Yeah, whatever. I'll pass on that. When you gon' bring her ass around and stop hiding her?"

He rolled his eyes. "You've seen her before," he told me.

"When? Where?"

"She was here at the house that night. You talked to her and everything."

"Nigga, I was zooted as fuck that night. I don't remember shit but Elite givin' me back that fuckin' ring."

He shook his head. "Yo, how about you just focus on yourself and gettin' your family back together, aight?"

I shrugged. "I don't know. Maybe I got one last try in me, but if that shit don't work, I'm done."

SAVANNAH

"You've got to give me something, Savannah. They think you can't do your job," Shep told me.

"Look, I know you've been covering me by trying to throw a few bones my way before we go to meet with the chief, but—"

"Yeah, and I'm getting tired of it. I'm so close to nailing these guys, I can feel it. Now that you've been in his house, have you heard or seen anything?"

I shook my head. "No. Nothing that you probably haven't seen."

He eyed me with suspicion, and I shot him a serious look. "I'm being honest. I don't know. I told you. I don't see that side of him."

"Well, get me something, anything. I've been working on his cousin. I have a meeting set up with him and some under-cover DEA agents later. I wanna nail this mothafucka's head to the wall."

"You make it sound so personal."

"Look, a lot has changed since the last time we talked."

I folded my arms across my chest. "Like what?"
"Just know I was wrong when I told you some people weren't worth saving."
My eyebrows knitted together. "What do you mean?"
He shook his head. "Nothing."
"Look, Shep. I know I don't know you that well, but don't do anything crazy."
"I know what I'm doing and the risks that come along with it," he assured me.

There was no doubt in my mind that Shep could handle himself when it came to doing whatever he was conspiring in his head to do. He'd proven to me that I wasn't the only one who was addicted to the burn I felt when playing with fire.

"I just want this to end peacefully," I told him.

"And it will, for some of us."

His words left an eerie feeling in the pit of my stomach. As soon as we parted ways, I caught an Uber to Pharaoh's house. He'd been begging me to accept the car he randomly surprised me with, but I kept turning him down. The morbid conversation I had with Shep weighed heavy on my mind as soon as I stepped inside. I was grateful that Shep had offered to cover for me because I hadn't gotten any information for them to use against Pharaoh. I knew it was my job to get him to reveal the dark side of himself, but I didn't want to see it. I liked him just the way he was. He walked over to me and kissed my forehead.

"What's wrong?" he asked me.

"Nothing."

"Why you lyin'?"

"Why don't you let me in?" I asked him.

"What do you mean? I have let you in."

"No, I mean really let me in. Like, why don't you ever tell me about what you do all day when you're not with me?"

"Look, I know what you're getting at, so I'm going to stop you right there. I don't want you knowin' shit about that part of me."

"Why not?"

"Because I care about you enough to never let you see that side of me."

"What if I told you I wanted to?"

He searched my eyes for any sign of fear or uncertainty. "Once you step over into this shit, there ain't no unseeing it," he warned.

"I'm ready. Remember how you told me that you wanted to get to know me inside and out?"

"Yeah."

"Well, I want to know you inside and out, too."

Chapter Fourteen

FRENCHIE

Elite agreed to let me come over and watch the kids while she got herself together to run some errands. I was sitting downstairs, watching cartoons with Imani, when Paxton started crying. I rocked his swing, and he started getting fussier.

"Yo, Elite, where is Pax's pacifier?" I yelled upstairs.

"It's in his room!" she yelled back.

I scooped Paxton into my arms and walked upstairs to find his pacifier. I rocked him as I looked in his room and didn't see it. I headed into the master bedroom and opened the door to the bathroom. "Elite, you said it was in his room, but I don't see —"

I paused until my brain registered what my eyes were seeing. "What the fuck are you doing? Are you pregnant again?" I asked, staring at the pregnancy test in her hand.

Her eyes widened. "Get the fuck out, Frenchie!"

"No, fuck that. Are you fuckin' pregnant again?"

She looked down at the bath rug underneath her feet, and I walked over and snatched the test from her hands. I walked back into the bedroom, laid Paxton on the bed, and then read the test. I turned to look at her with a serious look on my face. "How far along are you?"

She shook her head. "I don't know."

"Fuck you mean you don't know? You got two of my seeds. You know your body."

"I said I don't know, Frenchie! Damn!"

"What you mad for? You don't want to have another baby with me?"

She frowned. "No! I don't want another baby period! We have two kids, and we're not even together now! Fuck I look like bringing another life into that?"

"Whose fault is it that we're not together, huh?" I asked, reminding her that she was the one who gave me back my engagement ring.

"Are you seriously asking me that shit right now?"

"Yeah, you trippin' like I'm not gon' take care of my baby."

"It's not about that."

I blew air out of my nose. "For a second, I thought you were about to tell me that it wasn't my baby."

Her forehead creased. "What the fuck are you talkin' about?"

I shrugged her off. "I'm just sayin'."

"Nigga, you know better than to ask me some shit like that. You're the one with maybe baby twins on the way, not me!"

"Yo, what the fuck I tell you about that shit, Elite? They not mine!"

"I don't care what you say anymore. Baby or not, it doesn't change shit between us. I'm done with you."

"You would tell me if it wasn't my kid, right?" I asked.

"What?"

"You heard me, Elite."

The unstable look on her face and her trembling voice sent a wave of paranoia crashing through my system. I quickly seized her by the throat, stifling her voice. "If I didn't love you so much, I swear I'd mothafuckin' kill you."

I released my grip, and she fell to her knees. She screamed as tears ran out of her eyes like waterfalls. I stepped over her and headed toward the front door.

"Frenchie!" She yelled my name over and over, pleading for me to come back.

"Fuck you, Elite! And if I find out your ass been sleepin' with another nigga, I'll kill both of you mothafuckas!" I yelled and slammed the door behind me.

My blood was boiling, and I was ready to kill a nigga. Whatever nigga rubbed me the wrong way when I was in my bag must've had a death wish. I couldn't believe Elite's ass. She was lucky I didn't kill her ass. It was always the disloyal mothafuckas that wanted to play the mothafuckin' victim.

I knew I had a hand in pushing Elite's ass to the edge. No matter what I did, she would always be my lil' baby, but she was changing. The shit I was on could've had my mind playin' tricks on me, but love or not, I would take her soul if she broke my heart.

PHARAOH

I opened the door for French and turned to make my way back into the kitchen where I was heating up some leftovers. "What up, nigga?"

He looked at me and sucked his teeth. "Elite is pregnant again."

My eyes widened. The last thing Frenchie needed was another mouth to feed. "Oh shit."

"I know, right. What the fuck I'm gon' do with four fuckin' babies?"

"Start wearin' a condom, nigga."

"Pussy too good, nigga. I can't."

He chuckled, and I shook my head with a smirk. "How y'all doin' anyway?"

"Nigga, we not. To be honest, I think she been fuckin' around."

"This shit again? Nah, not Elite."

"I swear! I can't prove it, but it's just a feelin' nigga. I could see it in her eyes."

"With who?"

"I don't know. It could be somebody or nobody. I swear to

God she drives me crazy. I hate her ass, but if anybody tried to harm her in any way, I would rip a nigga's throat out for her."

"Y'all got that crazy love."

"I know. But peep this. What's up with your boy Rico?"

"What you mean?"

"The nigga actin' funny. He came to me about settin' up a meetin' with some niggas that could get us double the product for less than what we payin' to get it now."

My eyes narrowed. "Fuck outta here."

"Exactly. I knew that shit ain't sound good when he told me about it, but I told him to set it up anyway just to see how he'd act."

"And? What happened?"

"I get with the nigga, and we ride out to the meeting spot, and I start feelin' crazy inside like everything in my body is tellin' me this nigga tryna set me up. So we get there, wait for thirty minutes, and then he tells me they not comin'. I'm like yo, I gotta get back to the city, so he drops me back off at the crib and shit like everything cool, but it ain't."

"You think he talkin' to the feds?"

"Either he talkin' or he is one. I don't know, nigga. I'm not feelin' his ass no more. I knew my hunch about his ass was right all along, but we need to make sure we know what team that nigga really on."

"Only one way to find out. Take 'em to the spot."

"What the fuck you wanna do?" French asked me as he sparked his blunt.

"Talk to him, see how shit sounds. If it don't sound right, then I'll handle that nigga, permanently."

"And if he is talkin' to the feds?"

"Whatever started with him will end with his ass, too. Ghosts don't talk, mothafucka."

Frenchie nodded and turned to leave. I could tell from the look in his eyes that he wasn't all there. He was on the verge of a breakdown and was probably going to kill somebody. I walked upstairs and woke up Savannah, who was laying naked in my bed.

"Wake up. I want you to ride out somewhere with me," I whispered to her.

Chapter Fifteen

ELITE

I swung the door open and froze. The number one person I had been trying to avoid was standing at my doorstep. "Rico, what the fuck are you doing here?"

"What you mean? What's up, Elite? Why you not answerin' my phone calls all of a sudden."

"You shouldn't be here."

"Just tell me what's up, and I'll leave, I swear."

Although I knew French was nowhere in sight, I still didn't want to risk him catching Rico anywhere near me. Not after what went down between us. "Look, I just don't want to talk to you right now."

"Nah, fuck that. I'm not buyin' that shit. You pulled that shit the first time you got uncomfortable."

I shook my head. "Rico, please just go," I said, fighting back tears.

"Not until you tell me what's up. Either that, or I walk

away, and we never speak again."

Silence hung in between us until he turned to leave. "I'm pregnant," I whispered to his back.

He quickly turned back around to face me. "Are you sure?"

I nodded as I wiped the tears off my cheeks. "I'm sure... And before you ask, it's yours."

He eyed me closely. "So what do you want to do?"

My forehead creased. "What do you mean? There's only one option, Rico. I already have two kids and a fucked-up relationship. Why would you even want that type of life with me?"

He ran his hand over the back of his head. "Look, the last thing I expected to happen was for it to go down like this between us, but we're here now, and I'm a grown ass man, Elite. I don't know what you're used to, but I ain't gon' cry over this shit. If we havin' a baby, then we havin' a baby, together. Please don't try to deny me or yourself of that."

"What do you want from me, Rico? Shit is not that simple. Frenchie knows."

"You told him first?"

"I didn't tell him at all. He walked in on me when I was taking the fuckin' pregnancy test."

"What did he say?"

"He went off," I said, lifting my neck so he could see the red marks.

"That nigga put his hands on you, Elite?"

I shook my head. "He's never done it before, okay? Just calm down."

"Fuck that. I'm not gon' calm shit down!"

I held my hand out to his chest. "You don't have to save

me, Rico. This is my life. It's not like we can run off and be to-gether. I have kids here, a business... a family."

"You can do hair anywhere. You know that."

"I want to do it here. I have clientele here. My entire life is here in Chicago."

His mouth frowned. "You sound scared."

"Fuck you! I'm not scared. I just sat here and told you why I'm not leaving!"

"Fine, then you're too comfortable."

"I have two kids, Rico! Two! Now with this pregnancy makes three if I keep it. I can't just throw my shit in a bag and get up and go when I feel like it, even if I want to sometimes."

"There it is right there. It's not that you can't leave, you just don't want to."

"It doesn't matter what I want. I'm just playing with the cards I was dealt, okay?"

"What if I told you that you could switch hands?"

"What?"

"Elite... There's something I need to tell you."

"What is it?"

Right before he opened his mouth to tell me whatever it was he needed to tell me, his phone rang. The factory iPhone ringtone blared loudly as he pulled it out of his pocket to an-swer it.

"Hello? What's up? Yeah... Aight, bet. I'm on my way." When he hung up the phone, he looked at me with a serious look in his eyes. "I have to go, but I'll be back to tell you everything, I promise."

"O-okay."

He quickly kissed my lips and darted out of the door.

SAVANNAH

"Meet me at the spot now. It's important," Pharaoh said to someone over the phone and then hung up.

"Who was that?"

"French."

"Is everything okay?"

"It will be. I just gotta go handle something."

Pharaoh pressed his foot on the gas, and we zoomed through Chicago doing no less than ninety miles per hour. My nails dug into the sides of the seat as I braced myself for impact because I just knew he was going to kill us both with his reckless driving.

"No seriously, where are we going?"

"I told you I need to handle something."

"Could you be more specific?"

He quickly took his eyes off the road and shot a look in my direction. "You askin' a lot of questions."

My eyebrows raised. "Because you're speeding down the highway like a maniac, and it's scaring me!"

"Look, I got word that somebody in the camp might be talkin' to the opps, and I'm gon' handle it."

"Wait, like an informant or something?"

"A mothafuckin' rat."

My eyes widened as I looked down at the gun sitting in his lap. "Who is it?" I mumbled.

"Don't worry about it. I won't be long."

The car fell silent, and I could feel the nervous energy bouncing around inside my body. There was no way he could've known about me or Shep, but then again, I wasn't sure. We pulled up to a large abandoned building on the outskirts of the city, and he shut the engine off.

"Stay here," he said and slammed the door.

As soon as he got out of the car, I slipped my hand inside my purse and dropped my location to the chief. Then, I took a look at my surroundings and saw Shep's car haphazardly parked off to the side.

"Shit," I mumbled.

My heartbeat pounded so hard inside my chest it felt like it was going to break through the skin. I frantically looked around the car for a gun, knife, or any other weapon I could use before getting out of the car and walking into whatever it was they were doing inside the warehouse.

The moment I stepped out of the car, I heard yelling. I quickly ran up to the door and tried to look inside. When I realized I couldn't see anything, I took a deep breath and opened the door. My eyes immediately widened at the sight of Shep tied up to a chair. He'd been severely beaten. One of his eyes was swollen shut, and there were bruises and lacerations on his face with caked up blood on them.

"Oh my God!" I yelled, then quickly covered my mouth.

Pharaoh and his cousin both looked up at me. One wore a smile, the other a frown. "I thought I told you to stay in the car," Pharaoh told me.

"What are you doing in here? Stop this shit right now!"

"Get the fuck out!" Frenchie yelled at me. "Let's hurry up and finish this nigga, P."

I watched Pharaoh turn away from me while pulling his gun out from behind his back. "Is this what you wanted, huh? To bring this side out of me, nigga? I treated you good, let you into my circle. This is how you repay me, by talkin' to the mothafuckin' feds?"

Shep didn't say anything, and Frenchie drew back and pistol whipped him across the back of his head. As much as I knew I shouldn't have said anything, I couldn't stand by and watch them torture the man who was supposed to be my co-lead. I drew in a deep breath, knowing I would regret the words that were about to fly out of my mouth.

"Just tell him who you really are, Shep!" I yelled.

Pharaoh quickly turned his attention back to me. "Shep? How the fuck do you know this nigga?"

"I don't know her," Shep mumbled, trying to come to my defense.

"Move again, and I'll break your mothafuckin' face, nigga," Pharaoh said through gritted teeth.

"Yo, at this point, I don't give a fuck who the fuck this nigga is. It ain't gon' matter when they find the ashes of his fuckin' body in this bitch. Let's finish this nigga," Frenchie said.

Instead of listening to his cousin, Pharaoh turned his gun on me. I quickly stepped back and slowly raised my hands in the air. "How the fuck do you know this nigga, Savannah?"

"I—I..."

"Don't you fuckin' lie to me, Savannah! Or I swear to God!"

"Pharaoh, please..." I whispered.

"I'm only going to ask you this once, aight? Are you or are you not a fuckin' informant?" he yelled.

"I'm not! I'm not an informant!"

"Don't lie to me! Don't you fuckin' lie to me!" he said, shoving the gun in Shep's mouth.

"Please don't!" I trembled.

"Tell me the truth right now, or I'll blow his fucking brains out right here, I swear to God!" he yelled.

My chest tightened as my mouth gaped open. I couldn't believe what was about to come out. "I'm a special agent with the FBI," I said frantically with my trembling hands in the air. "And... Pharaoh Blackwell, you're under arrest."

To be continued...

A Note From the Author

Reader,

Thank you for reading the first installment of the *Fallin' for the Alpha of the Streets* series. Please, if you've made it this far, I hope you'll consider taking a minute to tell me what you thought about the book in the form of a **book review**. Don't hesitate to let me know what you'd like to see from me next! I thoroughly enjoy reading your reviews and hearing from you as well! I'm always striving to attract new readers and retain current ones, and reviews are one of the easiest ways to attract readers. If you loved the book, tell a friend, and most importantly, let me know!

All my love,

KL Hall

About the Author

As a serial storyteller, K.L. Hall pens enthralling love stories intertwined with the grittiness of urban fiction. Her writing style is a fusion of eminently relatable female characters like Sydney Tate and Raquel Valentine, and the flawed, yet desirable male leads who love them, like Law Calloway and Justice Silva.

Highly Acclaimed Series:
In the Arms of a Savage: (Peaked at #1 in Women's Fiction)
In the Arms of a Savage 2: (Peaked at #3 in Women's Fiction)
In the Arms of a Savage 3: (Peaked at #2 in Women's Fiction)

Text KLHALL to 22828 to sign up for my mailing list to stay up to date with new releases, giveaways, sneak peeks and more! Connect with Me on Social Media:
Facebook: K.L. Hall https://goo.gl/yGP59B
Twitter: @authorklhall
Instagram: @authorklhall
Website: www.authorklhall.com

Up Next: Fallin' for the Alpha of the Streets 2

Other novels by K.L. Hall:
Diary of a Hood Princess 1-3
Rise of a Street King: The Justice Silva Story *(Spin-Off to the Diary of a Hood Princess series)*
Where He Belongs: A Disrespectful Love Story
Love Me Harder: A Sin City Love Story
Broken Condoms and Promises 1-3
In the Arms of a Savage 1-3
Built for a Savage: Blaze and Camille's Love Story *(Spin-Off*

to the In the Arms of a Savage Series)
A Ruthle$$ Love Story 1-3
Fallin' for the Alpha of the Streets 1-2
The Most Savage of Them All: The Wolfe Calloway Story
(Prequel to the In the Arms of a Savage Series)
When a Gangsta Loves a Good Girl

Novellas:
Bi-Curious: An Erotic Tale
House of Cards
A Savage Calloway Christmas *(Christmas novella to the In the Arms of a Savage Series)*
Lovin' the Alpha of the Streets: A Valentine's Day Novella *(Valentine's Day novella to the Fallin' for the Alpha of the Streets Series)*
Awakened: A Paranormal Romance Novella
Caught Between my Husband and a Hustler

www.ingramcontent.com/pod-product-compliance
Lightning Source LLC
Chambersburg PA
CBHW020910180626
46816CB00007BA/2331